THE END OF THE CENTURY

David Rolland

Jitney Books

#MADEINDADE

#MIAMIFULLTIME

To You

September 2, 1999
Prologue

"Why do you want to work at Borders?"

"I have rent to pay. And food. And gas I guess for my car."

"Okay. What assets will you bring to the team at Borders?"

"I'm really hard working. For a bookstore I'll seem hardworking I figure. And I'm opinionated. I mean if someone comes in here and wants a book to read or a CD to listen to I'll get them what they didn't know they needed."

"Oh great. What prior work experience do you have that can prepare you for the Borders Bookstore environment?"

"I've had lots of jobs. I wouldn't even know where to start."

"You can start with your first job."

"I delivered newspapers as a boy. I worked at a pumpkin patch one Halloween. Oh, and at college, this is probably the most similar experience to working here, I worked at the school library."

"Wonderful! So you have some experience picking out the right books for people?"

"I was more responsible for dusting the books and shelves and making sure no one was smoking or having sex or anything in the back, but yeah sometimes people would ask where a book was and I'd help them out. And I wrote for a newspaper at the school. They paid $15 an article. It's not much, but it seemed kind of cool to get paid to write."

"Very cool."

"I still write for them actually. It won't interfere with the work here. They're in Davis. In California. I e-mail them my stories. And I guess that's it. I mean I figure you just want to know the jobs I paid taxes on, you know that there's a record of, not under the table type stuff?"

"No."

As she wrote things down and refused to look at Matt, he began to panic. This was the fifth job interview over the last two weeks. His bank account was on fumes and he did not want to have to drive cross country back home so soon after telling everyone sayonara suckers. On the drive east to Miami, he figured everything would finally fall in place. Thus far that was not the case.

"You graduated from college?"

"Yes. UC Davis back in May. Top of the class. Not the very top, but you know high up there." Matt had to stop himself from asking questions. Jay had told Matt everything he was doing wrong at his previous interviews at the *Miami Herald*, at the *Key Biscayne Islander News*, at Miami Dade Community College. He had been too honest. He hadn't been boastful enough about himself and too boastful about his ambitions. Employers wanted to hear this was exactly where he wanted to be and he was exactly who they needed, so he added, "You know, I think I'd be a really strong addition to the team at Borders."

"Great. Did you want to work full-time or part-time?"

"Full-time. I'm kind of broke. Full-time."

"Okay. Fantastic. We have an opening as a lead manager."

"Manager?"

"Yes. I think you'll be perfect for it. You earn $7.50 an hour instead of $6. You're responsible for giving all the floor staff their fifteen minutes breaks and you check the employees in and out when they come in. How does that sound?"

"So, I'm hired?"

"Yes, welcome to the Borders team. Our dress code is cas." He had no idea what "cas" meant until she added, "You can wear shorts or t-shirts or tennies if you like. We're going to have an orientation with our other team members on Tuesday at 1 PM. So, they'll see you then?"

"Great, I'll see you then."

"I'm not going to be there."

"No?"

"Uh-uh. Tomorrow's my last day. Time for bigger and better things. But I'm sure you'll love it here. Good luck."

THE END OF THE CENTURY

August 1, 1999
It Begins with a Single Step

Matt was trying his best to get drunk. Drinking was what you did when your heart broke. At least that's what popular culture told him. Matt didn't like the taste of beer and especially wasn't into the foul power of hard liquor. Instead, he drank a third pint of pear cider. The carbonation took some getting used to, but it reminded him of juice and he was starting to feel a little lighter, a little freer.

By the time Jay came in with a stack of quarters and invited him to the pool table, Matt said, "Why the hell not?"

After sinking the eight ball in to lose the first game and then scratching on the break to disqualify himself in the second, Matt was finally starting to find a flow. He was stripes and sunk an easy shot, followed by a more challenging bank to feel comfortable going for a tricky angle. He was shaky with the cue though and his shot missed badly. "Fuck!" he said quietly and then louder. "Fuck!"

Jay just laughed. He laughed so hard his next shot scratched.

Matt took time lining the white ball exactly where he wanted. He managed to sink the next target only for the cue ball to slowly droop in as well. "Fuck!" he yelled louder than ever.

Jay laughed. He'd known Matt since freshman year, they were in the same dorm. They had a couple late night chats. They'd always been friendly, though never quite friends. This was out of the character that Jay knew. "Everything going okay, Matt?"

"Yeah. I mean no. I fucking missed the shot."

"I'd never heard you yell before."

"Well, I don't give a fuck any more." This caused Jay to laugh even harder. "I'm leaving this shit hole. They can all remember me as a yeller, a guy who yells fuck whenever he misses a shot. I don't care."

"Where are you going?"

"I don't know. As far away as I can. Some place where nobody knows my name and I don't know anybody."

"Like Miami?"

"Yeah or like fucking Scotland or China or somewhere."

"How about Miami?" Jay's wheels were turning. "I have an uncle there who always said I could stay with him. I'm sure you could stay there too."

"That's really far."

"Isn't that what you wanted?"

"Yeah, alright. Let's go."

"Right now?"

"Fuck it. That's how you do it. Just do it or it doesn't get done."

"There's a lot of truth to that, Matt. But I have to pack and call my uncle and quit my job and that takes time."

"I don't have time. Every time I see her face it kills me. I don't have too many lives left."

So that was it. Jay rarely saw Matt without his girlfriend, what was her name? The redhead? The two of them had been together since sophomore year. Jay realized right then if he wanted to get to Florida he better move quick. These first loves rarely ever break up forever ever. The two of them will be back together if he allowed them too long. "Give me a couple days, Matt. Thursday at the latest."

"Thursday? Thursday I guess is a good day as any to be the first day of the rest of my life."

"So, would that make Wednesday the last day of this life?"

"I'm in between lives. This is Purgatory."

August 4, 1999
The Short Good-Bye

Matt was at a loss. He was behaving cowardly, but also knew there was no other way. The morning after Erin told Matt she cheated on him, he said flat out he was leaving. But he continued to share the bed with her, even twice making love and hate together. Since the break up not much had really changed in their day to day living. She went to class, he went to work at the school library, or to the local paper to type up his assignments. They ate from the same refrigerator, bathed from the same shower, the only difference was the resentment and animosity that moved into the apartment.

Since Jay put Florida in Matt's head he wrestled with how to tell Erin he was leaving. So, he didn't. He told his boss at the library, he told his editors who kindly said he could still write for them from any spot on the globe through the miracle of e-mail. He told both his friends who were still in town for the summer, but he didn't tell Erin. Part of him thought she deserved to just come home and see all his things gone, but then part of him also wanted to hurt her and see that realization in her face that he was actually leaving.

"Good-bye," she said.

"Yes, good-bye and have a good life."

She rolled her eyes at that and he figured he was going to let her come home to an empty apartment. It wouldn't be that empty since everything in the apartment was hers. But his clothes wouldn't be there and neither would he. But by some miracle as if she was telepathic or clairvoyant or at the very least empathic, she said, "This isn't good. I don't think we should be like this. If we're really breaking up, maybe you should go?"

"You'll be happy to know I am going."

"Where? You're going to stay with someone else?"

"That's what I'm going to do."

"You're going to stay with Kevin or...?"

"No. I'm leaving town. I'm leaving Davis. I'm leaving you."

"You're going to go home to your parents?" Matt had considered that option as an alternative to the great unknown of Florida, but he had the terrible choice of falling in love with someone who shared the same hometown. Erin was a grade behind him at Palo Alto High School. They didn't really know each other then. He noticed her like he would any pretty girl, but they didn't speak or associate until they saw each other around the campus of the university they both by either coincidence or fate decided to attend and became entwined. Palo Alto would flood back all those painful, heartbreaking emotions just as much as Davis would. All of Northern California was tainted, all of California really. And England too. That's where she cheated on him the first time during her semester abroad. She waited to tell him until he came to visit. After an awful week where Stonehenge was forever ruined, they decided to stay together and work things out.

"No, I'm going to Florida."

"Florida? By yourself?"

"No, with Jay. He has an uncle he said we can stay with."

"Who's Jay?"

"You know, Jay with the shaved head that I play basketball with sometimes. He came by one time to borrow your Doors CD."

"The pothead Jay?" she realized. "When are you going?"

"Today. Now."

"Fuck you," she said, shutting the door. He was going to chase after her. Beg her forgiveness and ask her to marry him, but she came back in. "I didn't even hardly do anything. All I did was kiss the guy."

He loved her more than anything or anyone in the world. He hated her more than anything or anyone in the world. All these conflicting emotions paralyzed him. He didn't kiss her, he didn't hug her, he didn't even say the words "good bye". He let the tears fall out of her eyes and his and she left. He packed his bags and fit what he could in the back of his station wagon. Then he drove cross town to pick up Jay.

August 7, 1999
On the Path

The Grand Canyon was worth the detour. It made the hole in Matt's heart seem insignificant and meaningless. For that he was grateful. The upper rim was filled with sightseers. Were they all also in such desperate need for proof that there was beauty and majesty and vastness in the world?

Jay suggested they walk to the bottom. Matt agreed since there were too many people around on the hot summer day for him to really appreciate the moment. An hour into the descent was when Jay first hinted maybe they should turn around. They kept going. Then Matt suggested that they seemed no closer to the bottom then when they started. Still they continued. When a line of burros carrying people down the trail left behind a souvenir of shit that was more green than brown that Jay almost tripped into was when they accepted they were ill prepared for such a journey.

Still it was beautiful. Matt figured if there was any truth that right before you died your life flashed in front of your eyes, the Grand Canyon would make that cut. After they got some quarters to pay for their first shower of the trip, they got back on the road. They tried their best to save money by taking turns at the wheel of Matt's Peugeot station wagon all throughout the night insteading of splurging on a roadside motel. On the I-40 through New Mexico and into Texas they talked.

Jay spoke about Miami as they passed sagebrush. "Until I was eleven we lived on this island called Key Biscayne. They used to sell bumper stickers for cars that would say 'Key Biscayne Paradise Found'."

"It sounds nice."

"Yeah, in my head I remember all these cool things. It seemed like a magical town, but I don't know if that's just me romanticizing the past before my parents got divorced and my mom moved us to California. So, in my head I'm thinking paradise found, sandy beaches, little banks that give out popcorn on Fridays and have a haunted house for Halloween. But then if I think harder I can feel little cracks, you know, like my parents screaming at each other, me getting beat up by other kids, and my third grade teacher who used to pull on my hair when she didn't like an answer I gave her."

Matt kind of envied Jay in the way he put himself right out there. He would tell people anything no matter how personal or none of your business it was. Matt felt quite the opposite. On their Grand Canyon hike before the sun got too hot and Jay was too tired to speak he was pressing Matt on what happened with Erin. "It wasn't working out," was what Matt told him at first.

"It wasn't working out because she cheated on you?"

"It's more complicated then that." It was, but it was also easier than that. He was 22 and she was 21. They had been together for two and a half years. Hers were the only lips he'd ever kissed, well besides his relatives. But she was exclusively the only woman whose body he'd ever seen and touched and penetrated and there were times when he hoped that would always be the case.

There was also a part of him that wanted to see the world. Maybe that's why she felt the need to come home late at night in tears. He was not the jealous type. He thought nothing of it when she decided to go meet some friends who she had met on-line playing some weird computer game. They had met up before and he even met the crew. They seemed like nerds, dorks, geeks. He never imagined there could be some attraction. But at 4 in the morning, she confessed of a kiss and another kiss. It woke him up in pure anger. Matt and Erin fought and blame was assigned and divided and at 8 in the morning he told her, "I can't do this any more."

"You know Ponce de Leon discovered Key Biscayne?" Jay asked.

"Cool." Matt said as he kept his eye on the road.

"You know who he was, right? The Spanish explorer."

Matt didn't care. He was a little peeved at how mundane the scenery was. He wanted to take I-10, but Jay persuaded him that the 40 was a better route. I-10 hugged the Mexican border and they could bother you and detain you for no reason at all. Matt thought it would be cool to maybe check out Mexico. He'd been to Tijuana with his family when he was a kid and remembered the donkeys painted like zebras fondly. But Jay confessed he had a couple joints in his backpack.

When Matt said he thought the joint they smoked at the Grand Canyon was the only weed he had, Jay was quick to respond that's what he thought too, but when he went to brush his teeth he saw there were two forgotten remnants in his backpack. It didn't seem that outrageous to Matt since Jay was one of University of California's Davis branch's busiest marijuana dealers. Inventory could slip through cracks.

So instead of Las Cruces and El Paso and San Antonio, they went through Albuquerque and Amarillo.

"In 1521, Ponce de Leon went to the island. He got attacked by the natives and took off. He put Key Biscayne on the map though and that island became a regular stop for all the other European explorers and conquistadores to stock up on fresh water. But maybe that's not why they all stopped there. Because you know what Ponce de Leon is most famous for, right?"

Matt didn't answer. He was going to try to get some shut eye. He gave up on seeing any UFO's that lady at the gas station said were so frequent that locals pulled up on the side of the road to sit in lawn chairs to watch the flashing lights and strange stellar objects in the night sky.

"That's right, the Fountain of Youth. Finding that was old Juan's main goal in life. Maybe he found it. I tell you if it's there, I'm going to find that sucker too."

August 10, 1999
Realization

They arrived at Uncle Jim's Fort Lauderdale house at night so Matt couldn't experience fully what he had gotten himself into. The much too soft couch was fine for his exhaustion so he slept long and hard. When the sun crept through the shades was when he realized the filth he landed into. The smell of bacon frying was overwhelming as though they were running a diner. Matt sat up and saw Jay nowhere around. Uncle Jim though was a meter behind him, scraping the skillet with a spatula as though there was gold at its core.

Uncle Jim made eye contact through his glasses. Matt felt it rude not to be cheerful. "Good morning," Matt said.

Uncle Jim turned back to his breakfast.

This was not the hero's welcome Matt had expected. It was, he felt noteworthy that they made it from one side of the country to another in five days. He didn't necessarily need a parade, though that would be nice, but this was just rude. Last night as they pulled into Uncle Jim's front lawn, Matt was really looking forward to a bed. They'd slept in the car except for that one night they got an awful motel outside Pensacola.

They brought their bags to Uncle Jim's door and Jay knocked hard. No answer then he knocked harder. That was when Uncle Jim came to the door. A short, white haired man, who Matt later found out was actually Jay's grandfather's younger brother. With his shirt off Uncle Jim looked at the two travelers with no apparent clue of who they were.

Jay did not allow this moment to be awkward. He went in for a hug and started rat-a-tatting in Spanish, a language, Matt had always eschewed as an elective in both high school and college. A smile came to Uncle Jim's face which abruptly disappeared when he looked and nodded at Matt and spoke some more mumbo-jumbo.

Jay spoke some more words Matt could not comprehend, but Matt heard his name said, so he stuck out his hand for a shake. Uncle Jim did not accept it. He said something though which caused both he and Jay to laugh. Jay picked up his bag and waved Matt in, "Come on."

Matt walked into the house where the roar of a wall air conditioning unit was at full blast. They passed one room with a television set broadcasting news in Spanish and were led to a living room. There were two couches. "You can take the big one." Jay said. They looked the same size, so Matt just chose the couch that was closest.

"Can I use the bathroom?" Matt asked. There was no acknowledgment as uncle or great-uncle and nephew conversed in a foreign language. Matt walked toward the open door from which he could see a sink. He turned on a light. One little bug scurried away. Was it a cockroach? He wasn't exactly sure, though Jay had warned him they were everywhere in Florida.

What concerned and creeped out Matt slightly more was a cut out four-foot pinned on picture of a smiling leprechaun. As Matt took care of his business and brushed his teeth, he was a little worried of where he found himself. In this day and age didn't everyone know leprechauns and clowns were no longer considered friendly faces, but rather omens for insanity and depravity?

Matt spat out the toothpaste and turned off the bathroom light. He could now hear Jim and Jay were conversing in the international language of arguing. Matt was exhausted. At this moment of homelessness and uncertainty they would have to drag him out of here, so he took out his sleeping bag and made the couch a bed for the night.

Matt closed his eyes. Eventually Jay and Uncle Jim stopped arguing and Matt could hear a door slam shut. He saw Jay was setting up his sleeping bag on the couch. "What the fuck, Jay?"

"I swear to God the guy lost his mind. Last week I called him and told him I was coming with a friend."

"I didn't know you spoke Spanish."

"Come on, man, my Dad's Cuban. Where do you think I got my name?" Before Matt could question whether Jay was actually a Spanish language name, he was filled in on Jay's birth name. "Jose Rasco."

It was amazing how little Matt knew about Jay or Jose. Jay was an expert of talking about anything but the obvious. Matt was now fully versed on the Fountain of Youth and the various spots on Key Biscayne where this supernatural fluid might be flowing, but he hadn't learned enough details on where they would be sleeping. But this he supposed was how adventures went.

It would be disappointing if there were no unexpected surprises. That's what Matt told himself before he fell asleep. But as he rolled up his sleeping bag in the morning everything seemed more real. Jay was nowhere to be seen, so he said to his host, "Thanks again for letting us stay here." No response. Uncle Jim sat down and began tearing into his breakfast. He had a hardcover book he began to read. On the front cover was Pope John Paul II. "The Pope. He's a great guy." Still nothing. Matt asked, "Do you know where Jay is?"

Uncle Jim pointed at the front door. "OK, I'll leave you then to your book. Have a good day."

It was so goddamned hot outside. Hotter and stickier than anything he ever imagined. Matt had nowhere to go and nothing to do when he remembered to call his parents and let them know he made it. He drove down the street and found a Denny's a mile down. He walked to the pay phone before he realized the time change. It was 6 am in California. So, he bought a newspaper, sat in a booth and ordered breakfast. There was a man across the restaurant that he could swear did not have a nose. Where the nose should have been was a bandage. Matt tried to get a good look, but every time he did the man would look up.

Matt flipped through the newspaper and headed straight towards the classified ads. This is the adult thing to do he told himself. He had $1,200 in his bank account enough to give him some breathing room, but he needed a job and most likely an apartment. The waitress asked if he wanted anything. He figured it was only right to order the pun filled "Moons over My Hammy" sandwich even if it doesn't sound too appetizing. He scouted around the restaurant to see the man without a nose staring at him.

So, he looked at jobs. It was slim pickings. Lots of sales. Selling knives, real estate, retail. There was a demand for truckers and paralegals. Many of the jobs required knowledge of Spanish. He saw the newspaper was hiring, but only in the advertising department. No writers, no reporters, no editors. Matt was a good proofreader. He always checked Erin's papers before she printed them out and never failed to find mistakes. Maybe he should call her? It was kind of rude to not give her warning. They were more than lovers, they were also roommates. Perhaps he should have paid September's rent as well?

His food came and Matt devoured it. He looked at the apartments. The cheapest he saw was $400 and required first month, last month, and deposit. That was all the money he had. What was he thinking? He wasn't thinking. He just felt he needed to do something. He was 22 and had only even kissed one girl in his life, so he packed his stuff and drove off with a guy who left him at his crazy uncle's house.

The man without a nose got up. Matt stared. He had no nose, he was certain of it. Well, he figured, he could now say this new part of his life had some meaning. He drove across the country to see if one could survive and even eat breakfast without a nose. Halfway through his meal Matt decided to take his time. He had no place to go now. Or ever in fact. His future was completely blank.

He read through every item in the paper. He studied the baseball box scores. He looked at what movies were playing and what time *Friends* was on TV here. He read what mischief Garfield got himself into. Then he did the crossword puzzle. Boris Yeltsin had fired his entire cabinet. A gunman wounded five and killed one at a Los Angeles Jewish Community Center. There was a total solar eclipse in Europe and Asia.

This was ridiculous Matt thought. He paid the check and walked out to his car. He got in the driver seat. It was so hot. It burned the bottom of his legs. It never seemed worth the money to get his air conditioning fixed. Now it seemed like one of the three biggest mistakes of his life. But Matt drove. He had gotten good at driving. He headed east which didn't take him too long to get to the end of the road. He was at the beach. He parked his car and walked. Then he turned around and dug out his hat. The Indiana Jones hat he bought in New Mexico.

He took off his shoes, but the sand, the white sand was also hot. Everything was hot. Ft. Lauderdale, Florida. This was the part of the world you go to when you want to melt. The ocean was not much cooler. It was shallow and seaweed washed on to shore. Matt looked down the coast and saw what appeared to him to be people walking on the water. Was this the land of miracles where the supernatural exists?

He walked towards the figures until he realized they were walking on sand flats. Little islands had popped up due to the lowering of the tide. Some teenagers were throwing boards at the sand flats, chasing after them, and then jumping aboard allowing their weight to glide them as far as possible. Matt thought it looked fun and considered asking them for a try, but by the time he got close, they were heading out. He was alone.

This was it Matt figured. He had made it to the end of the line. There was nowhere further he could drive. What a mistake. He had it made. He had friends. He had an apartment. He had not one, but two jobs. He had someone he loved, someone who loved him.

Then he noticed a tiny isle forming toward the horizon. He walked out towards it. It was circular, the size of a studio apartment. This could be his new home. He would never leave. He would fish and occasionally ask some skimboarding kids to fetch him a coconut. He sat down on the clammy sand and laughed at this possible future. There were a thousand of them, a million of them, possibilities. He looked around at his little domain and saw the sea was already encroaching.

He wondered if this was the reason he had driven so far. Without his presence no one would have ever known this island existed, even if it only existed for the briefest of moments. But now this island would not be forgotten, it would be remembered and loved even as it disappeared. Matt knew there was truth to this idea, because as soon as he finished that thought, a wave covered the island for good.

August 11, 1999
Everything Changes

"Where did you go?" Jay yelled before Matt could get his Peugeot into park.

"I went to the beach."

"All day? All night?"

"Yeah pretty much."

"You slept on the beach?

"I slept in the car."

"You're crazy."

Matt wasn't so much crazy as he was a liar. He had found a motel that had a room for $60 a night. It wasn't the cleanest of locales, but he watched HBO all night and wasn't woken up by the smell of bacon. "Don't do that again without letting me know. For all I knew you got killed or robbed and left for dead. This isn't Davis or Sausalito. It happens all the time here." Matt didn't have time to correct Jay that he wasn't from Sausalito. "Come on, let's go, I want to show you around."

They jumped back in the car. Jay pointed toward I-95. "For now on when you venture somewhere let me know. At least leave me a note."

'You were gone when I woke up."

"I was in the backyard. There's a mango tree. I picked a bunch. When we get back you can have some."

Matt decided to bring up the touchy subject. "I don't think your uncle likes that I'm there.'

"Uncle Jim seems like an asshole, but he's a pussy cat. What's that saying? He's all bite, no bark?" Matt didn't correct him this time. He learned from their drive that Jay liked to rearrange clichés. You can't judge a cover by its book. Whatever makes you stronger, doesn't kill you. "He's cool for us to stay a little while. Cousin Alex is kind of weird though. You haven't met him yet. While you stranded me there and had me waiting around all day and night he finally came out. Poor guy I think is overmedicated. He just stays in that room on-line and reads *Spawn* comic books all day."

Was he doing this on purpose? Trying to make things even more awkward during his stay? But at least this cousin Alex explained one thing. "Is he the one who put up that leprechaun in the bathroom?"

"That's weird, right? I don't know. I think it's from when Uncle Jim used to own a cake shop. He'd make cakes for weddings and birthdays and that sort of thing."

They made their way out of Broward County down to Coconut Grove. Jay explained that when he moved from Miami, this was the place to be. At least for the middle school kids. Every Friday night one parent or another would drop them off there. They'd see a movie or wander into a shop or see if they ran into some other kids they knew.

Jay almost fell backward when he saw the Hooters restaurant was still in business. "One time we must have been fourteen and me and two friends got a table and ordered French fries. The waitress sat down with us. You know how they dress, right? In those tight orange shorts and low cut shirts so that everyone can see why they gave the restaurant its name. Our waitress, at the time she must have been the hottest woman in the world. It was dead and she just sat down with us and asked, 'You guys go to University of Miami?' One of my friends told her we were going into high school. I wanted to kill him. We thought he messed up our chance with her. It's funny how it's hard to get back in that mindset. What did we think she would do with us? Did I think she would have sex with all of us if we were college students? Well, now I'm a college student. A college drop out at least. Maybe we should go have lunch there?"

Matt was game, but Jay said he had to run an errand first. He told Matt to walk around and in an hour they would meet at Hooters. Matt checked out Cocowalk. It seemed like nothing more than an outdoor mall. He found a pay phone and decided to use his calling card to make a few calls. He spoke to his parents. He assured them everything was great. It felt very humid, but it was where he was meant to be right now. Then he called Erin. The answering machine came on and Matt hung up. He called her again. "Hi Erin, it's me. I made it. We went to the Grand Canyon. All the way to the bottom. It was beautiful not as beautiful as…" he stopped himself. "But yeah we made it to Miami. Things are good. I hope things are good for you. Okay, bye."

It wasn't one of the best messages Matt had ever left, but he wasn't going to make it worse by leaving another one. Matt got to Hooters a little early. It was fairly empty. Both waitresses were scantily clad. Neither was the prettiest woman in the world, that would be Erin, thank you very much, but they were pleasing to the eye.

"Sit anywhere you like," the dark haired one said to him. Matt took a table by the balcony under a ceiling fan. He watched from the third floor as the cars drove by past the Johnny Rockets retro '50's diner. A little further he could see the ocean, or what he would later learn was actually Biscayne Bay. "Can I get you something to drink?"

"Do you have cider?"

"No," she said. "Here is our beer selection." She pointed at the menu in a way that Matt had no choice but to stare at her cleavage. That was intentional, right? Maybe getting over Erin wouldn't be as difficult as it seemed. Or maybe she does that to every customer for a tip? "I'll just have some water. I'm waiting on a friend."

"Yo, yo, yo." That friend was here. He patted Matt on the back. It seemed Jay had put a strong dap of marijuana cologne all over his body. "Did you order yet?" before Matt had a chance to answer Jay said, "Get whatever you want. It's on me." He then handed Matt three bills. $300. "Here's the gas money I owed you. I told you I was good for it. I finally got it all straightened out with my bank." Matt was spacey, but not autistic. He knew Jay was not at the bank getting his finances straightened out. The one night where they got a motel room outside Pensacola Matt had searched Jay's bags while he was in the shower. And in his traveler's backpack Jay found a box of Potpourri inside of which were several tightly packed zip-loc bags of marijuana.

They devoured their lunch and Matt had a question. "What are you going to do now?"

"I figured I'd continue giving you the grand tour. I want to show you Key Biscayne where I grew up."

"No, I mean beyond today. Now that we're here in Florida and you got your money, what are you going to do?"

Jay relished receiving this question. He did everything but clap his hands in fulfillment. "See, thinking beyond today, that's where you and most of society get it all wrong. Today is all we are promised. Yesterday is gone and tomorrow never comes, it's always just out of reach, a day ahead of you, the dog us carrots keep chasing." Jay got up to signify the end of his stoner wisdom class. "Come on, let's take a drive down my memory lane."

Jay was hazy with the directions, but eventually he found the road he wanted to go down. He was amazed how little Bayshore Drive had changed in the seven years since he last drove down it. The truck selling frozen lemonade was still parked on the side of the road. He pointed out the Museum of Science with the Planetarium. Then they cut a right and saw a three-dimensional model of a shark advertising for the Miami Seaquarium. Jay made a big deal about how he would cover the $1 toll to get over the bridges.

"This is Florida," Matt thought as they headed uphill over the mile-long bridge. Downtown Miami with its skyscrapers on one side while the glassy blue sea faced the other. They kept driving. Over another bridge, past the wooded expanse of Crandon Park and then they hit the town. Jay quieted as he looked around, ready to jump on any difference from his memory. They reached a flat park with a children's playground. "This is new. This was just trees before." Jay told Matt to make a right and pointed out his old school. "There were these two old ficus trees. Hurricane Andrew knocked them down. They used to have these metal bleachers we'd use to climb into the tree." Jay continued the navigation, right and then a left and then: "What the fuck! Stop the car!"

Matt did as commanded. Jay stepped out and watched as a plot of land was being constructed upon. There was no need for explanation. Matt could imagine this was where Jay once lived. Jay got back in the car. Matt drove. Even though Matt's parents had lived in the same house since before he was born, Matt could relate. Our pasts, the things we believe to be the sturdiest are constantly changing. Our pasts are disappearing, being razed and built over.

Matt took one turn and then another. He figured since they were on an island he couldn't get too lost. They reached a gas station when Jay began navigating again. "Make a u-turn here." They pulled into Calusa Park. There were four tennis courts and a little concrete shelter. "What the fuck?" Jay said staring at the wild grass. "There was a tiny little playhouse here. I think it had been here since the '50's. My sister and I were in a play. We were munchkins in the Wizard of Oz." Jay kept walking. Matt followed him through a sandy playground. There was a four-story caged metal structure with a slide meant to approximate a rocket. There was a boat play structure anchored on the sand complete with ladders and poles and a steering wheel. They walked past a set of swings into the trees.

"At least the mangroves are still here." They walked on a muddy path dodging spider webs. "We used to sneak back here whenever we could. We said there was a ninja training camp. The older kids, teenagers on Key Biscayne that called themselves Key Rats used to hang out in the mangroves. Our parents warned us to stay away from them. It made my mind wonder what they did in here. They were probably just drinking stolen beers and having sex."

Matt tried to sympathize he really did, but as he skipped from one puddle over another and after his hand got bloody from swatting mosquitoes he was ready to get out of this mess. Eventually they arrived where they couldn't walk any further. The water was knee high. Jay took a seat on a tree trunk and whipped out a joint. Matt sat down.

"Want to know what I'm going to do now we're here?" Jay took a puff for the ages before passing it on to Matt. "I'm going to find the Fountain of Youth. I know it's here. I'm going to search every square inch of this fucking place until I drink from it."

August 16, 1999
Home

It was the fourth place Matt had looked at. He had been picky up to this point. The first house Matt checked was affordable. A bearded, divorced Dad wanted to rent out an extra room now that his daughter was off to college. It was clean and the guy seemed nice enough, but Matt had the feeling that if he invited a girl over for a home cooked dinner, his landlord/roommate might come in with his shirt off to watch television and say, "Don't mind me, I'm just checking out the game."

The second place was a studio on South Beach. It was spotless, with hard wood floors, a gas stove, and three blocks from the beach. Matt told the lady who showed it he would take it right then and now. She said, "Why don't you fill out the application and I'll get back to you?" She never did. Matt figured it was because he brought Jay. She was insistent that there was only one resident who could live there and Jay kept asking her question after question until she wondered, "Who is the one who wants to live here?"

The third apartment, also on South Beach, was a mess. Stained carpet, grease on the oven, and for some insane reason Matt would have to provide his own refrigerator.

But this morning Matt felt a sense of urgency to find his own place. It had been nearly a week that he had called Casa de Uncle Jim home. But this morning as he tried to sleep in as he knew no other way to fill his empty days he could hear Uncle Jim say the word "Maricon." This was a dirty word in Spanish and while Matt could not completely rule out that Uncle Jim was directing that crude word to someone else, chances were pretty damn good it was directed toward the guy he did not know staying uninvited on the couch where he usually read his Spanish language biography of Ronald Reagan.

So, this Coconut Grove apartment, as long as there was not the outline of a body would be home. Matt parked his car on the street and walked up the stairs to the third floor. He knocked and a guy his age wearing glasses answered. "Matt?" he asked. "I'm Gabe, come on in."

Matt entered. The air conditioning was on strong. The living room, and in fact the entire apartment was kind of a dump, but a big dump. There was a balcony with a couch on it overlooking the neighborhood. They walked down the hallway and into the bedroom furnished with a mattress on a box spring and a wooden desk. "You can keep or throw out whatever you want. It's $350 a month and a $350 deposit. You can move in whenever you want and we can just prorate this month." Matt tried to envision this being where he laid his head.

Matt was shown the bathroom. The tile was dirty enough that he knew he would never take a bath in this tub. "This here is John's room." Gabe said pointing to a closed door.

"There's a third roommate?" Matt asked.

"Oh no, it will just be you and him. I'm moving out. I graduated and landed a job in New York." Perhaps Matt's face showed concern on why his new roommate was not giving him the tour because Gabe explained. "Don't worry, John's cool. You'll hardly see him. He works at a computer lab at the University of Miami at night and sleeps most of the day. Sometimes he'll sleep out in the living room and watch a movie. He's big on *The Matrix* now. That's probably the only time you'll ever see him. So yeah man, if you like it just let me know."

"I like it," Matt said.

"Okay. Cool. You want to give me cash? A check?" Matt handed him the cash he had and said he would write the check for the rest. Gabe asked, "When do you want to move in?"

"I have my stuff in the car downstairs. Can I move in now?"

"Yeah. Let me just clear some of my last stuff out and here's the key, enjoy."

The whole transaction seemed rather rushed, haphazard, and possibly illegal but during his short orientation to Florida that seemed to describe every one of his interactions. Matt went downstairs to collect his bags, his little boom box and CD collection as Gabe removed a house plant and a computer.

Matt looked into the closet which was empty except for a black Brooks Brothers suit and a sports coat. Matt tried them on, they fit almost perfectly. He looked at the desk, solid wood. He could do some great writing here. The bed had sheets on them, Matt was about to strip them until he realized he had no sheets of his own. He was exhausted. The stress and the heat had tired him out. He collapsed on the bed still wearing the pants of the suit. The bed was perhaps the most uncomfortable object in the universe. He could feel on certain sections the points of dangerous springs, while other parts of the bed seemed ready to collapse if he ate an extra slice of key lime pie. It took him ninety seconds to fall into a deep sleep.

August 18, 1999
Stranger

There was a phone in the house. Attached to it was an answering machine blinking a red digital number three. Matt looked down the hallway at his roommate's door. It was closed shut. Maybe this mysterious person he was sharing a roof and walls with was sleeping, maybe he was out? Matt figured he would check the messages. Perhaps one would be for him, however unlikely that might seem since Matt had never given anyone the phone number partly because he himself did not know his phone number.

The first message was from a creditor seeking to speak to John Randall Suarez. The second number was an automated message from a creditor telling John Randall Suarez to please call them back. Finally, there was what seemed to be a wrong number as it was spoken very quickly in Spanish. Matt turned on the television. He was unsure what to do with himself. He had enough money to pay September's rent, but after that, what? He switched from one station to another and then he pulled out a paperback he bought at a used bookstore in Texas. It was Tom Robbins' *Even Cowgirls Get the Blues*. He'd heard someone speak fondly of the book once and he knew there was a movie with Uma Thurman playing the title character. Matt always had a crush on Uma. He tried to see the protagonist as her, but a few pages in Matt's eyes got heavy. He tried to power through and keep reading, but eventually his eyelids won. Then a door opened waking Matt right up. He was utterly discombobulated not exactly sure where or even who he was.

A round man, with brown hair slightly receding, dressed in a black t-shirt and jeans drenched in sweat entered holding a bag filled with fast food. Matt collected himself. "I guess you're John. I'm Matt. I'm your new roommate. Gabe showed me around and I gave him his deposit and the rest of the month's rent and I'm here taking his place. I just moved here from California a week ago. I really like it down here." Matt was unsure how long he was going to keep going. Maybe until this stranger said something? He figured he should ask a question that required an answer. "How long have you lived here?"

"Three years," said John, in a way that almost seemed like a question.

"You must really like it here, then?"

"Yes. Yes, I do."

Matt tried not to judge, but he was uncertain from John's extremely flat affect whether he might be some sort of robot meant to simulate humanity, only without proper emotional programming. But then he remembered John worked nights, maybe he was just exhausted. "Gabe told me you work at night at a computer lab?"

"Yeah, I have a couple jobs. I work at the University of Miami working on their IT. I also have another job, but I'm not allowed to tell anyone about that."

"That's cool. So, you work for like the CIA?"

"I can't talk about any of that." John put his head down and headed towards his room.

"It was good meeting you, John."

John nodded holding the bag oozing of grease as he headed toward his bedroom. All Matt could think about was "What the fuck?" He drove thousands of miles for this? He felt as lonely as he had since the preceding day when he did not speak to a single soul. He would remedy this. He picked up the phone and dialed Erin's number. He thought he could be strong but that was a mistake. It was her answering machine. "Hi Erin, it's Matt. I made it to Florida. I have my own place. I don't have a phone number, well I do, but I don't know it yet. I just wanted to hear your voice, I guess. I'm sorry if I said mean things to you before I left. I didn't mean them. Well, I did then, but now I don't. Okay. I'll try calling you later and hopefully then I'll know the phone number so you can call me back."

Matt took his keys and decided to go for a walk. Get some fresh air, familiarize himself with the neighborhood, maybe find something to eat. As he entered the humidity, Matt couldn't help but feel like a disappointment. Here he was free to go wherever he wanted, do whatever he felt like doing, no responsibilities, no obligations, and he took the easy way out, settling down at the first decent place that would have him. Maybe Erin was right to seek out someone else. She had often complained he had no passion, no drive, was too complacent. Boy, had he not shown her.

It was strange though how she felt like more of a presence in his mind when they were apart, then when they lived together. Her absence was a ghost haunting his every move and making him regret every decision. He almost thought of ending it all. He could step in front of a truck as it went full speed and put an end to this monotony of heartache once and for all. Or maybe he could call Jay? See if he wanted to do something?

August 22, 1999
Another Player

Matt marveled at how Jay was able to climb so high. The palm tree had no branches to use as rungs, but yet here he was fifteen feet closer to the sky picking coconuts. Matt tried to follow Jay's method of taking off his t-shirt and tying it around his ankles to give himself more leverage. But Matt didn't have the upper body strength or the fearlessness or something to pull himself upward.

Jay however had that quality and was grabbing one green coconut after another off the tree and throwing them down. This was a good idea. Matt had become fearful the first of the month was coming closer and he had no prospect of income. Jay said all you need to survive is a coconut. Inside those hard to break shells are every nutrient you need except for Vitamin D and that's something sunshine will provide.

"Hey, what are you doing?" a bearded man yelled out of a white pickup truck. As he drove closer, Matt could see it said Dade County Park Services on the driver's side front door. "What are you doing?" the guy repeated as the truck came to a full stop as close to the tree as the asphalt would allow.

"We're building a treehouse."

The driver looked so confused that Matt felt obliged to tell him the truth, "We're getting coconuts."

"You can't do that."

"Why not?" Jay asked as he slid down the trunk.

"It's against the law."

"Fine," Jay said as he started picking up the coconuts on the grass. Matt followed his lead.

"You can't take those."

"Why not? We already took them off the tree."

"You want me to call the police?" The man said as he pulled out his walkie-talkie as though it was a weapon of mass destruction.

"Fucking fascist," Jay said. Matt started walking and Jay relented to do the same though he continued his complaints. "What a dick. Acting like he owns the place. This is public land, it belongs to the people."

Matt looked back to see the park employee eyeing them as they walked across the marina to his car. Fortunately, it took six trees before they were discovered, and he had forty-four coconuts in the back of his station wagon. Matt saw the park employee picking up the remaining coconuts and sticking them in the flatbed of his truck. He figured for the sake of peace he wouldn't point out this hypocrisy to Jay.

Matt was hungry. Under the shade of a sea grape tree he worked on digging towards the flesh of the coconut. He learned after their first harvest how to properly and easily defeat the coconut's steely rind. Instead of smashing it against the concrete hoping it will crack and when it does losing valuable water, take a screwdriver and dig at the mulchy end until you reach softness. Then you could use a spoon to get to the edible portions. But first, drink your reward, the sweet nectar inside the coconut. This diet wasn't going to help keep his weight, but at the very least Matt figured it was making his trips to the bathroom regular.

"Maybe we can wander the beach and sell these?' Jay said. "I've seen guys do it. We'd just need some fancy looking straws and I bet tourists would pay five bucks a pop."

This was both what was intriguing and annoying about Jay. He always had an ulterior motive, one that was usually secret that remained unrevealed until the last possible moment.

Better to focus on the positive, Matt figured. They had a good laugh this morning when John entered the living room. Matt and Jay were watching a rebroadcast of a ten-year-old basketball game on one of the upper echelon cable channels. As an adult Matt had not been much of a television watcher. But with empty days he had devolved into his childhood habit where his parents could plop him in front of a TV to waste away hours.

John came in and watched the game for a moment like it was nothing he had ever seen. "This is interesting," he said.

"Are you a basketball fan?" Matt asked.

"No," John said. He watched intently for a moment. "I wonder what would happen if you threw another ball into the game?" he asked as Michael Jordan dribbled past three Detroit Pistons.

Jay looked at Matt like what the holy hell. Matt though did not want to offend the person he shared the apartment with so he acted like that was a completely rational question. "Well, you would have two games going on at once."

"Hmm, that's true. I guess the kind of games I play are different." The three men who either by fate or by circumstance happened to be sharing the room and the conversation at the moment let that comment sit for a long time. Then John walked towards the door adding for good measure, "Well, I'm off to play in the tournament."

The rest of the afternoon the two friends made wild stabs of what kind of a tournament John was involved in. Their guesses went from the rational, some kind of role playing Dungeons and Dragons type tournament to the ridiculous like a hard boiled egg eating competition, into the absurd, like that John was an alien life form involved in some contest whose outcome would decide the fate of human civilization.

Matt enjoyed these types of conversations with Jay. It kept his mind from wandering into depressed states. His long awaited telephone conversation with Erin did not go as well as he hoped. It was painful and humiliating. At first it was awkward. There were apologies from both sides and forgiveness. Then the rhythms of their dialogue became fluid, like flirtatious chatter between the two good friends they had become over the years. In fact, it started to go too well. Matt felt the freedom to suggest, "Maybe I could come out there to visit you? I could buy an airplane ticket? Or maybe you could fly out here? It's different here. It's hotter than anywhere you've ever been, but you'd like the beach. The water is like a bathtub and you can sunbathe topless."

Unlike his earlier sexy talk, this time she didn't reciprocate. She stayed quiet until offering, "I don't think that's a good idea."

He was going to ask why not, but the worst, basest, most jealous parts of him instinctively knew, "You're seeing that guy? You're with that guy you kissed?"

"I'm not with him, I'm just, it's good we're apart right now."

"We are apart."

Was it a question, it certainly wasn't a declaration since Matt spent the last moments of their phone call pleading with her to change her mind. Even before they hung up Matt knew this was what heartbreak felt like. He'd often thought the answer to the song was that being the owner of a broken heart was much better than being the owner of a lonely heart. Now he realized that assumption was all wrong.

August 27, 1999
Hungry

Matt thought the interview went well. A neighborhood weekly newspaper was looking for a writer to cover local news. Matt explained he was new to the area and with a fresh eye he could really give their readers a unique perspective. The editor seemed to like him, so he was certain that it was only a matter of time before he could have a steady pay check and could afford to eat something that wasn't a coconut.

With money on his mind Matt walked into Borders bookstore, a massive two story complex of all things printed material as well as CD's. The only income Matt was able to continue to pull in was $20 a week from continuing his comic book column for *Diversions*, the Davis, California entertainment weekly. Matt preferred to focus on indie cutting edge comics, but rent was due in five days and he couldn't be careless buying anything. He went upstairs to the store's graphic novel section and picked a trade paperback of old Krazy Kat comics. Matt sat on the floor and figured he could pull out 400 words on the subversive, anarchic wit from yesteryear.

Yesteryear.

It had Matt thinking about how in the cool air conditioning, it's almost like he never moved. There is a Borders a mile away from where he grew up that from the inside could be nearly identical from the place where he currently sat. The rows and rows of books, the employees lazily ambling around shelving product, the skinflints like him, who use these superstores as libraries, with libraries now being used solely to check your e-mail and write and file your weekly comic book column.

As Matt passed the information kiosk, he couldn't help but notice a sign that said "Borders is now hiring" and next to it a stack of applications. For a second Matt was about to grab one, but then he thought how pathetic. Here he was thousands of miles away from where his story began and he was going to work at a place identical to where he once lived? Matt figured he should challenge himself and work a profession unique to his location. Maybe on a charter fishing boat or at a Cuban coffee bodega?

He went to the magazine rack and settled on an issue with an autumn movie preview. He brought it over to the café section and perused through it as he sat at one of their tables. Matt was excited to see one of his favorite video directors was going to release his first feature film in October. Oliver Stone had a football movie coming out that was shot in Miami. They're making a new version of *Fantasia* as well?

He looked up to see two women getting up from their lunch. They picked up their bags and their book and left behind a plate with a barely touched croissant. Maybe they took one bite out of it. Matt stopped himself from succumbing to whatever pangs of hunger that were tempting him. To do what he was thinking was bum behavior.

He went back into the future. Winona Ryder had a new movie coming out where she was in an all women insane asylum. They were releasing a new Sleepy Hollow with Johnny Depp as Ichabod Crane.

Why weren't any of the workers cleaning that table? The customers had obviously left. Matt looked. No one was watching him. Even if they were watching, nobody knew him. Beyond that what did it matter what they thought of him for eating someone's food anyway.

He stood up, but as he approached the table he lost his nerve and walked right past the croissant. This was no way to live he figured. Instead he walked to the job applications and picked one up. He went toward the exit to head to his car and grab his pen, but on the way laid the croissant. This time he picked it up. The plate almost dropped to the ground, but settled on the table. No one was the wiser.

He ripped off the bread that was bitten and then took a bite.

It was stale.

August 31, 1999
Wet

"It's been a long time since I've been on a date."

"You're doing fine." The blonde woman in a tight sweater said to him as she held his hand.

Matt figured now wasn't the time to correct himself that he had actually never been on a date. The romance with Erin sprung out of familiarity and happenstance. There were no planned appointments over dinner or movies where they figured out they were smitten over each other. The blonde smiled at him. She looked like a movie star, or maybe it was someone on TV when she smiled at him. He couldn't quite place her. The way she smiled was friendly enough that he felt comfortable asking, "Would you mind if I kissed you?"

"You better," she said. Then she rushed him like a lioness toward her cubs. Matt realized that metaphor wasn't quite right as her tongue rammed into his mouth. He didn't quite care at that moment. What he was more concerned about as she pressed her body against his was that he would not be able to control his body for much longer. Her flesh and touch were making it impossible to hold out. And then as she sighed deeply into his ear... BOOM

He woke up to find he had made a mess of himself. Again. This had been happening way too frequently. He wiped himself off with his shirt and wondered if these nocturnal emissions were happening because his body had become used to regular doses of sex and now nothing, but his seed still needed out.

He'd have to do the laundry again. These rolls of quarters added up. There was nothing he could do about the humidity causing him to change his clothes twice a day because of accumulated sweat. This other bodily fluid was not a luxury his budget could afford.

Matt opened his door to run to the bathroom. He was embarrassed to hear the television was on and someone might see the wet spot on his pants, but then he realized it was John passed out on the floor with a blanket over his head as he replayed a videotape of old *Simpsons* episodes as background noise.

He showered himself off soaping up the appropriate spots. As he dried himself off he stared into the mirror as the steam slowly evaporated. He could see his face. Had it been three days since he shaved, four? This was the look of a pathetic man. He made himself a promise as he looked into his own eyes, if he was not happy by his next birthday he would find the strength to kill himself.

Then he realized his birthday wasn't all that far away. To commit to something with the finality of death he should give life a bit more of a chance. He settled on the birthday after next. If he still felt this despair at twenty-four, then there would be no hope and he would say goodbye to this existence forever.

With that settled Matt dried off and put on his clothes. He was starving. He was hungry when he went to bed at two in the morning, but figured that would be a wasted meal since he was going straight to sleep. There was a place he had learned of from John. A little Nicaraguan spot where they would fill a giant styrofoam container with rice and beans and plantains and some kind of vinegary shredded cabbage salad for the insane price of two dollars. Matt thought about driving, but it was only a couple miles away and what else did the day have to offer? A couple blocks into his walk he regretted his decision. It was so hot. The sweat was starting to build. He even thought a rash began to develop on the inside of his thigh, so he tried to walk bowlegged.

As cars drove by and he looked for shade to make the walk more pleasant Matt began to feel ashamed. Why was he feeling this way? He had no job, no responsibilities, he could do whatever he wanted. It was his imagination that was letting him down. Instead of paying rent tomorrow he could take that money and put it toward his gas tank and head to New York. He had a friend there who said Matt was welcome any time he wanted to stop by. He had a cousin in Brooklyn too, so he could couch hop and not get stuck looking like a lecher like he did with Jay's uncle. There was also the possibility of a cash infusion from selling his car. He could head out to Europe. He received that e-mail from Jared telling him how unbelievably cheap Prague was. Behind the Iron Curtain could be where he finds himself.

A loud clap of thunder beckoned in the horizon. Matt knew moving wasn't an option. If this month long sojourn had taught him anything so far, it's that geography doesn't solve anything. You can't run away from your problems, because as far as you roam, you're still going to be stuck with you.

He'll write that rent check and hit that interview at the bookstore in a couple of days. Maybe some structure will improve his life. Give him a reason to rise out of bed each morning, however trivial that reason might be. It also wouldn't hurt to earn some money so he wouldn't have to pinch every penny for whatever he could squeeze out of it.

He was starting to feel a glimmer of hope when he thought he felt a drop. It was more than a drop, it was now rain. Matt picked up the pace and began to run toward his two dollar lunch.

September 4, 1999
Nature

As they walked through the mangroves searching for the Fountain of Youth Matt decided now was as a good as time as any to tell Jay he was about to start working full time. He was surprised by Jay's response, "That's a good idea. I bet a lot of fine chicks walk in there."

"Yeah. Maybe if it works out I could get you a job there."

"Nah, I'm good with money right now." Matt looked at the photograph Jay had found that showed a helicopter eye's view of Key Biscayne, in hopes of identifying the direction of one of the hidden lakes it revealed. "But you know, maybe you could hook me up with a discount from time to time?"

"Sure, I think we get like fifteen percent off books and CD's." Matt's sneaker plopped into a thick morass of mud. The pain of cleaning it off would be an improvement. Last time they searched Matt wore flip-flops which allowed the red ants to bite him relentlessly leaving his feet covered in painful, pimple like marks. Many of the "lakes" turned out to just be temporary collections of salt water from the bay due to it being high tide, there were a couple actual bodies of water.

Matt was not about to drink from the primordial ooze that Jay was calling water. Matt pointed out that if Jay wanted to drink the stuff, he had a water purifier in his backpack he used many times on hiking trips with his Dad through the Sierras.

"What are you nuts, man? You might be purifying it from whatever magical properties it has." Jay went on partly to convince Matt, but mostly to talk himself into it, that any Fountain of Youth would more likely look disgusting. "Nature is gross. Youth is gross. You ever see a baby being born? That's not pristine. Placenta and blood are squirting all over the place."

Matt didn't think that was a very convincing point, but he didn't argue. Jay had a technique that he read about on how to drink water on whose safety you're not certain of. Submerge your hands in the water, lick each side, if it does not taste salty nor make your tongue itchy or swollen, you could try a small sip. The first time Jay did that he faked a seizure, although not very convincingly as he did not fall to the ground and instead squirmed around from a standing position.

Jay would always offer Matt a sip from every drop of water they found, but Matt always said no. Whatever powers the Fountain of Youth might bestow did not seem worth the risk of any of the thousands of water borne sicknesses.

"Do you feel any different?"

"I'm not sure." Jay was uncertain what exactly the Fountain of Youth would do to him. The most familiar telling was it would revive your body into a younger state, although with the wisdom of your experienced mind. Other accounts had it as a natural steroid, one that would give you vigor and energy. One theory was that the water was a hallucinogen taking your thoughts into a youthful, innocent state. "Try it. Tell me what you think."

Matt relented. His own choices were only leading towards misery. It was time to follow another's advice. He cupped his hands into the muck and licked. It was grainy, but no more disgusting than a shot of hard liquor. He decided to take a full sip. As soon as he swallowed he coughed violently. Vomit formed from his stomach, but Matt fought. After a short battle every drop he consumed stayed within his body.

Jay's face showed concern. "Are you okay?"

"No," Matt told him.

September 7, 1999
Orientation

Matt remembered from the interview that the dress code was "cas" short for casual, but figured he should look somewhat nice. Maybe there was a pretty girl working at the store? Plus, he was a lead manager, so he should appear somewhat professional. He settled on what he imagined he might wear on a first date, his newest jeans and a button down collared shirt.

The problem with having a car without air conditioning was apparent by the time he parked in the lot where he could receive validation. Matt was drenched in sweat. He walked to the public bathroom and stood in front of the mirror. He tried drying off his armpits with a dry paper towel, next with a wet paper towel he sopped up his face. Matt thought he looked like he just got out of the pool, but whatever, it was "cas" anyway.

Matt entered the front door with the idea that everyone would know who he was and where he should be, but as he looked around for clues on where to go, he realized he appeared to be just another customer. He walked to the information kiosk. "Hi, I'm Matt." No response. "Matthew Traxler. It's my first day working here."

"Hold on." The goateed man picked up a phone to his left. "Hi, some guy's here for his first day of work." He hung up the phone and addressed Matt. "Gary said to walk up the stairs and to wait by the children's section."

"Okay, thanks." Matt walked to the stairs and tried to remember what his duties were. Didn't the woman who hired him say as lead manager he was responsible for handing out breaks? If so, that rude guy who couldn't even bother to introduce himself would receive his break at half past never.

Matt climbed the stairs and perused the many volumes of Curious George. He didn't pick one of the yellow books up, but from a distance he marveled at the sheer diversity of stories about a single monkey. A man with his hair slicked back wearing a tie stuck out his hand. "Hi, Matthew?"

"Matt," he corrected him.

"Hi, I'm Gary. Come inside, we're just about to get started." Matt was escorted into a conference room. At a table sat a man who was bald except for an abbot's amount of gray hair on the sides and a woman in red framed glasses. Gary sat down with a clap. "Okay, good morning, we're all here now. Maybe we can start with everyone introducing themselves. My name's Gary, I'm a manager here. I've been working at this Borders location since it opened four years ago. Before that I was at the location further south on US1. Who'd like to go next?"

The older man spoke with a New York accent. "My name's Steve. I worked at Chimera Books the last twenty years until they went out of business last year."

"That was a great store," Gary chimed in.

Steve did not say anything to refute that, so the woman introduced herself. "Hi, I'm Sandra. I have an eight-year-old son and a daughter who just started kindergarten. This is my first time working at a bookstore. But I've worked retail for many years before I had children and I've always loved books. And music."

"Well, we have both of those," Gary said.

No one else was in the room, so Matt knew it was his turn to put his best foot forward. "Hi, I'm Matt. I just moved here from California. I really like it and yeah I like books too and music as well and yeah I always used to come to this store so it should be cool working here."

"Okay, great." Gary said and then handed out paperwork.

Steve put on reading glasses and looked at the papers very seriously. Matt figured he should do the same. They were just payroll forms. It took Matt a second to remember his new address, but the rest wasn't very challenging. Gary spoke about the do's and don'ts of their new job. The only words that stuck out were that you could not date your coworkers. Apparently, Matt's look of distress was noticeable since Steve said aloud, "Don't worry, you can still date customers."

There was laughter, even from Matt. They walked out of the room and were given the grand tour of the store. They walked through the children's section into the music section and were shown the bathrooms. Gary then took out a key card and swiped them into a room, that said "Employees Only." They toured the break room and were then introduced to a keypad where they would clock themselves in to begin every shift as well as clock themselves out at the end. They met other managers and an accountant who couldn't be bothered to even acknowledge them.

They walked downstairs and were shown the café and the various sections of books. They were each to pick a section to oversee that would be theirs to keep tidy and organized. "You're doing music though, right Steve?"

"Yeah," Steve said in his cigarette smoker's voice.

"Do you guys have preferences?"

"I'll do the art books." Sandra said in a foreign accent.

"I guess I'll do travel." Matt said.

"Okay, great." Gary picked up a loose book from the floor. "So, when you see a book or a few books laying around, don't put them back on the shelf. Walk them to the back where... oh no. Will you look at this?" Matt quickly scurried to see what was bothering Gary. There was a stack of four jewel cases that normally held CDs stashed on a bottom shelf in the wedding section. "Again. Someone keeps breaking these off and hiding them here."

Steve took a closer inspection at the cases. "Looks to me like someone burned them off." He pointed at a mark in the plastic which Matt agreed did look like burn marks.

Gary grabbed the cases. "Let me show you where they go." He led them through a double door past the magazines which Matt had never noticed. The drab room was huge. Punk rock played on a boom box at a low volume. "This is where everything gets organized. If you see a book or a CD bring it back here. A half hour before closing we pick all the loose merchandise and bring it here to be sorted. On your schedule every day you'll have an hour or two devoted to your section where you can put them back in their proper places."

Matt noticed where the travel section was and saw a wide assortment of paperback books about Guam and Brazil. The next stop of orientation was the information desk where they were told the proper Borders customer relations etiquette. If someone asks you for help in finding a book or section, don't point them in the direction, walk them to their destination until they were holding the book.

The trio were shown how to order books on the computer that were not in stock. They were told that if dealing with a customer in person and the phone began ringing, to say "excuse me" and answer the phone. This seemed counterintuitive, to the whole a bird in the hand was worth two in the bush philosophy, but it wasn't Matt's store.

They were taken to the cash registers and told they'd receive training for that later. They were shown the gift wrapping station behind the register which gave Matt more panic than any other of these new experiences. He figured he'd learn the gift wrapping craft or maybe he wouldn't. Maybe something better would come along first.

They were given a half hour break amidst their training to grab lunch. Matt bought and ate a forgettable sandwich on a park bench. On the walk back, he saw Steve smoking a cigarette leaning against the wall outside the store. Matt kind of nodded, but Steve initiated conversation. "What made you leave California to come to this hellhole?"

"It wasn't very thought out."

"You came here for school? A girl? It wasn't the weather."

"No, I graduated school and my girlfriend cheated on me. My friend said on Sunday let's move to Miami and on Thursday we were on the road."

This made Steve smile. "I like it. Be careful though, one day you blink an eye… how old are you?"

"Twenty-two."

"Twenty-fucking-two. God that's what I'm talking about. I used to be you. I was twenty one when I moved down here. I blinked my eyes and here I am an old man giving you advice to make the most of it."

"What made you move down here?"

"It was 1970. Every movie that came out, *Easy Rider*, *Midnight Cowboy*, it had the characters wanting to make it to Florida. I wanted to check it out. Anything had to be better than Jersey. I came down with my fishing rods and a basketball and now it's thirty years later."

"You must love it here."

"Yeah, either that or the sun melted my brain and I can't figure out which way to get out."

"Hey, guys." Matt turned around to see Sandra walking up to them. "Is this where training has moved?"

"Yeah, I'm giving life lessons 101."

"Ooooh I could use those." Sandra said with a smile as she put a hand in the back pocket of her pants. "I remember you at Chimera. You gave a good recommendation on a cook book."

"Glad I could be of service."

"I miss that store."

"I do too. But there's no room for the little guy. If you want a book or a record... excuse me, a CD, there's no room for independence. It's big corporate store or get out of the way." Steve put out his cigarette in the sole of his sneaker and finished his short monologue. "I think it's time for us to head back to train how to be part of the problem."

"Talking to him is a good way to encourage suicide, is it not?" Sandra asked Matt. "I think working here is going to be fun."

"I do too," Matt said.

September 11, 1999
Something Happens

It was Friday night. If you want to be precise, 12:30 a.m. Saturday morning. It was Matt's first time closing out the store as lead manager. He had to put a checkmark by everyone's name after making sure they weren't leaving with any store merchandise. He still was learning everyone's name. There seemed to be a limitless roster.

The final step after everyone left was to clock out alongside one of the actual managers. In this instance it was Dan. Matt was not fond of judging someone by their appearance, but Dan was perhaps the ugliest man he had ever been in close contact with. He was a big guy, a few pounds short of obese, and had facial features reminiscent to a warthog. But he was a jolly enough fellow, with the slightest hint of feminism in his Cuban accent. "I can't wait to get out of here," he said to Matt even though he insisted on taking the brutally slow elevator instead of one flight of stairs. "You must have some big plans?"

"No, I think I've got to catch up on sleep. This new schedule of working full time is going to take a little getting used to."

Dan made a raspberry noise with his lips. "Party pooper." They each clocked out and walked down the stairs.

"You're going to have a wild night out. I take it?"

"You never know." Dan said as his foot escaped from his flip-flop and scratched his massive tree trunk of a calf. "I'm always looking for interesting conversation." He checked off that Matt was borrowing from the store a copy of Albert Camus' *The Stranger*. They walked over to the alarm. Dan pushed some keys, there were a couple beeps and they quickly exited.

As Dan locked the glass door from the outside, Matt heard a voice that made him cringe. "Yo!!!!! It's Friday night, party night!"

Matt had to improvise. "Jay, what a surprise to see you. What are you doing here?"

"Have a good night," Dan said having gotten the picture.

Matt gave Jay a pissed off look. "You said I should meet you here at 12:30."

"Yeah, it's not your fault." They began walking toward the street where all the cars were in gridlock cruising through Coconut Grove. One car blasting music had hydraulics jacking the body of the car up and down seeming to break free from its wheels. "That guy wanted to hang."

"You should have brought him along. Next to him we both would have looked pretty suave."

"Yeah, I guess. He gives me a little bit of a creepy vibe."

"Even better. I'll tell you my philosophy which I'm going to start right now, right this second. I'm never going to say no to anything."

"Give me all your money."

"There's going to have to be caveats. I'm only saying yes to people who don't know that I'm refusing to say no."

"So, this new you would have gone out with Dan tonight?"

"I'm sure he had a lovely evening planned. It might have ended up with some cuddling and eating soft serve ice cream, but I'm sure it would have been enriching and I'd be a better man for it."

They jaywalked across some streets and settled into a dark bar called The Hungry Sailor. They stood at a table, Jay with his beer and Matt with his cider, and ogled at the women in their proximity. With each sip they were looking prettier and prettier. "Why is it so hard?"

"Right?" Jay agreed as they were on the same wavelength. "Look at these meatheads those girls are with. We're two much more awesome people. You can ask Dan, he can be our reference."

This had been their constant conversation since they left Davis, their loneliness, the lack of a feminine touch in their lives. Jay had been wary to encourage this kind of talk too much since it always ended in Matt pining for Erin. Jay would then have to remind him that she had done him wrong.

Matt stood up. "I'm going to introduce myself."

"To who?"

Matt looked around the room. There was so much beauty to choose from. He settled on two raven haired girls at the bar each wearing shoulderless tops. "Them."

"Do it. I'm two steps behind you."

Matt took a sip from his cup. He was grateful to have something in his hand. The cup was a crutch, it gave him the ability to move forward. He understood the appeal of cigarettes, suddenly. Whether it was subliminal or not, the lit cigarette symbolized fire and all the power, fury and destruction inherent in that element.

Matt stepped forward right next to the two women who were laughing amongst themselves. They were about their age Matt figured, but really who could tell. "Hi," Matt said. There was no response. The music was loud. So he said it again louder looking right at them. "Hi." He knew they heard him, but they were acting like they didn't. He smiled at the shorter of the two, she turned right around. Matt put his cup on the bar, and acted like returning his empty cup was his reason for stepping into their proximity at all.

He returned to Jay who asked, "What happened?"

"They said they both had boyfriends."

"Boring! Where's their sense of adventure? Whatever happened to people saying yes to anything you ask of them?"

They continued the night drinking and staring until the possibilities seemed to dry up. "When are you going to start working the register?" Jay asked as they walked on the sidewalk back to Matt's car.

"I don't know."

"Because there's some CD's I'd like that maybe you can get me a discount. I'm getting tired of…"

"Yo, what you doing lookin' at my girl?' They turned around to see a gangsta looking kid who was either in high school or just out of it sticking his chest out at Jay. They were surrounded by three of his friends.

"I wasn't," Jay said. Matt looked at the girl, of all the women they stared at this night, she definitely wasn't one of them. They were both into waifs in tight clothing and this was a woman euphemistically called "thick" wearing a loose fitting Polo shirt.

"You calling her a liar?"

"No." With that one of the kids pushed Jay from behind. Matt had a second to think. He didn't want to get into a fight, but he knew in that second that when a friend was pushed you had to have his back. So he shoved the kid in retaliation. Something hard hit the back of Matt's head. Matt managed to throw one punch and then found himself pushed toward an oncoming car. The car stopped and Matt saw Jay right by him.

The kids all started running away from them. Matt couldn't help himself. Maybe it was the adrenaline, maybe it was the suicidal impulses, but he started screaming. "That's right you pussies, you better run! You fucking pussies."

It was only then that Matt realized why they were running. The car that had stopped for him was a police car. "Get out of the street," the policeman yelled at Matt.

"Those guys just jumped us." Matt said pointing at the five figures running a block away.

"Do you want to come down to the station to press charges?"

"Can't you chase them? They're right there and they might attack someone else."

"You can come to the station and…"

Jay pulled Matt away. "We're okay. Thanks, Officer." As they walked back on their path toward Matt's car Jay asked, "What were you thinking talking to the cops? I have weed on me."

"I didn't know that. What fucking dicks."

"The cops or those pussies?"

"Everyone. You weren't staring at her, were you?"

"No. No more than I do to anyone."

This was when Matt recognized that Jay was holding the side of his face. It was already swelling up and turning purple. "Oh man, are you alright?"

"I don't know. I think they might have cracked one of my back teeth." Jay kind of surveyed the pain. "Thanks for doing that man. Not too many people would have stood up like that."

"You don't have to thank me. You'd do the same for me."

"I'd like to think I would."

September 13, 1999
The Coming Storm

All anyone wanted to talk about, the customers, the fellow employees, the television in the break room, was that Hurricane Floyd was on its way. In California Matt had felt his share of earthquakes. The one in '89 during the Word Series was the craziest. It lasted long enough that Matt could remember he thought he should leave the house, but by the time he finished the thought, the tremors were over. The epicenter was far away enough where there was no real danger.

Earthquakes came, they conquered, you licked your wounds and then dealt with the aftershocks. Hurricanes were something different. There was anxiety. How much damage would they cause? Should I evacuate? Should I just keep watching the weathermen and their forecasts for the foreseeable future?

"It's all a conspiracy." Steve said. Matt was a fan of conspiracies so he listened carefully as they took their mutual break. "Anytime there's a raindrop falling from the air these weathermen take over the broadcast. It increases viewership and it gets people buying like crazy at their favorite advertisers. Make sure to go to Publix to stock up on canned goods and bottled water. Get to the gas station and fill your tank all the way to full. While you're at it, visit Burdines and make sure you have your new Fall wardrobe ready."

"I heard Hurricane Andrew was bad."

"Yeah, that was the one. I didn't have power for a month. It didn't bother me too much. Air conditioning makes you sick anyway." Steve thought back to that summer of '92. "There's one good thing about hurricanes. If they say the sky is falling, we might not have any work tomorrow. It's the Florida version of the snow day."

"Tomorrow's my day off."

"Then you should really have yourself a hurricane party."

A hurricane party? Matt thought about that concept as he went back to his station at the information desk. He imagined drinking and dancing as the world gusted around him. One hundred plus mile winds as you twist and shout your cares away.

"Hey Matt, can I take my break," asked Cristina, the community college student with the tattoo of a cross on her forearm.

"Sure." He checked her off on the list and wrote the time 11:45. Then he incorporated her into the fantasy. Her hair was being blown all over the place. With a shrug of her shoulders she jumped into the outdoor pool. Matt dove in after her.

During Matt's lunchtime he learned from the store's general manager, Ken, that the store would be closing at 4. The store would also be closed the next day as well with further instructions to follow. Matt heard more stories about Andrew, how it pushed the boats in the Marina out of the water, how it gusted trees out of the ground and how it knocked over one of his co-workers houses so that she had to live in a camp called Tent City for her first semester of high school.

Matt volunteered to hammer sheets of plywood over the store's many windows. It took a while, but he thought he was getting the hang of it when Dan walked by to say, "You really don't know what you're doing, do you?"

"I guess not. I've never done this before."

Dan began breathing heavily as he held the wood in place with his left shoulder and hammered with his right hand. "Hold the hammer at the bottom of the handle, that's where you'll find your leverage."

When the store was boarded up and put into place, all the employees sat on the stairs as Ken addressed them. He told them to be safe and to call in tomorrow night to listen to the message and see if the store would be open. That information didn't matter to Matt. He had the next two days off anyway. As if to alienate him further from humanity his weekends were scheduled on Tuesdays and Wednesdays.

As Matt signed the workers out, he heard them sharing plans. He considered inquiring about what they might during their time off, but then figured he would appear needy or creepy, like a thinner Dan.

Matt went to his car and as the radio warned everyone to make sure they had food and water, he did what would have made Steve ashamed and went to the supermarket. The lines were long and the shelves were fairly bare. He bought some bananas and the only cans that were left that seemed somewhat appetizing in tomato soup. There was no bottled water, nor liquor of any sorts he was informed.

He got home and checked his answering machine. There was one message from his Mom making sure he was okay. There was another from Jay asking if he wanted to pick him up at Uncle Jim's. Uncle Jim was taping up the windows which Jay thought was insane, "A couple of x's of masking tape on your window is going to stop a natural disaster?"

Matt couldn't even be bothered to do that much. Should he at least bring the couch that was placed on their balcony inside? He was unsure. Maybe it would be best for him and everyone involved to let the wind and the rain and nature have its way. He turned on the tv. The woman in the tight dress in front of a radar printout of the storm spoke about fronts and probabilities. Matt made a couple phone calls. One was to his Mom. He left a message that everything should be alright. He was in a safe spot with plenty of tomato soup.

Then he called Erin. Again, he had to leave a message. "Hi, I don't know if you heard, but a hurricane is coming my way. I don't know if I'll ever have a chance to talk to you again. If I don't, I wanted to let you know I love you."

September 14, 1999
Disaster Averted

Matt woke up in the recliner to hear the door opening. He had evidently fallen asleep during the Monday Night Football game. His roommate John let himself in, for whatever reason Matt acted like he was not sleeping. He sat up as straight as the chair would allow. A weatherman was speaking on the TV, but instead of listening, Matt asked John, "How is it out there?"

"It's dark."

"No, I mean the hurricane."

"It's drizzling a little. There's wind, but I don't think there's a hurricane."

Matt went outside the front door. From the third story vantage point Matt could tell it was windy, very windy, but not perilous. He stepped back into the apartment and turned his attention back to the television. The weatherman with his rolled up sleeves spoke about how South Florida dodged a bullet. At the last second a front had pushed the hurricane off its projected path and was now veering north.

"All that talk and fear and it's just another day."

"A hurricane was supposed to come?" John asked. "I probably should be paying more attention to those kinds of things."

"It must be nice to have a job you like so much that you can just tune everything out."

"Yes, I take my work very seriously."

"I'd say so, you're up until..." Matt took a look at the clock on the VCR, "six am working. I'd say that's a serious commitment."

"I spend some of the time working, but mostly I play a game."

"What kind of game?" Matt was really trying to fish out what John's secret employment was, but he was fine with learning about what types of tournaments he was involved in.

"It's a capture the flag type game. You put on specialized goggles to give a three dimensional environment and you work as a team to try to capture your opponents." John went into finer detail about the specifics of the game, but Matt began droning out. John added, "I probably shouldn't play it as much as I do. Do you mind if I put this on?" John grabbed one of the video cassettes splayed out on the carpet and inserted it into the VCR.

Matt felt the need to ask, "How much do you play the game?"

"I've calculated that if you want to be any good at it, then you have to commit to at least forty hours a week."

"You probably could cut your playing time to half that and still be pretty good."

John kicked off his sneakers and put a little blanket over his head. "I find if I can't be exceptional at something, I get bored of it and decide not to do it at all."

"What else are you exceptional at?" Matt wondered.

"Skiing and dancing."

Matt decided not to question any further. He found some people are like onions, if you rip off one layer, you get to another layer that is equally strange, watery, and pungent. He tried to retreat into his bedroom, but the morning light was coming through his blinds and he couldn't find a way back into sleep. So, he walked down into his car and decided to drive to the beach. The streets were empty. Not even the usual newspapers were at the doorsteps.

He steered his car to the Key Biscayne toll booth. Matt had his dollar ready, but no one was manning the booth. Perhaps that was due to last night's evacuation order? Matt decided to save himself some money and drove right through. Some windsurfers were taking advantage of the weather and gliding along the choppy bay at a similar speed to what his car was going.

Matt parked his car where Jay had shown him, close to the only accessway to the beach that was open to the public. Matt left his shoes, key and shirt in the car, stretched out his legs a little bit and began running barefoot. Hurricane or not the waters had dredged up all kinds of debris on to the shore. Some of it was natural like the bales of brown seaweed, some of it was not like the bottles and plastic bags, some of it was toxic. There were the clear jellyfish, he had to make sure to dodge. Even more terrifying were the blue or purple Portuguese Man o'war whose stings were painful enough they were known to drive a grown sailor to tears. He did his best to elude them, but at one point he could have sworn he heard a pop beneath his foot. As the wind made his jog difficult, Matt had to question whether he was blessed. Even if his soul felt tortured and he often felt alone in the world, the Gods were on his side. Hurricanes avoided his path, jellyfish decided not to inject toxins into his skin. So, what if he loved Erin, with all his heart and she did not feel the need to return his call even if strong winds might have created their last chance to ever speak?

Maybe she was in the right to cut him loose. Maybe he had pushed her away without even knowing it? Maybe he had sent her signals that as much as he loved her, that he was not willing to sacrifice the world for her? He had his chance to do that, but instead of starting a family, he drove her to the clinic. It was her decision, he told himself many times, but it was also his. He would have sacrificed everything to start a family with her, really he would have. But it was the biggest relief that he didn't have to. The world and all its accompanying loneliness was now his to explore.

He did the math in his head as he often did of how old their child would be. A year. Julius if he was a boy, Destiny if a girl. They were sure she would be a girl, before they decided she wouldn't exist.

Matt made it to the end of the beach. The giant white lighthouse was as far as he could go. Jay had told him the lighthouse's whole history. It was one of the oldest things in South Florida surviving hurricanes and fires. The settlers fought a battle with the Seminole Indians and ran up to the top while the Natives tried to burn them all down. Matt didn't ask too many questions, but now he wondered how you could survive such a siege? Doesn't smoke rise?

Matt turned around and suddenly everything felt easier. The wind was at his back, pushing him faster where it once endeavored to slow him down. For a moment with nothing but piles and piles of seaweed in front of him, Matt could swear he was close to figuring something out. What that was, he was not sure, but he was close.

September 19, 1999
Marylise

"I hate this." Matt said aloud as he tried organizing the books in the back warehouse.

"What section are you in charge of?" Steve asked without looking up as he inserted the CD's into their protective plastic shells meant to prevent theft.

"Travel."

"Travel? Oh, that's a nightmare. Every jackass with a passport goes there to pull out a book to show their friend fancy places they've been and then they stick the book back wherever they feel like it."

Matt wondered why he didn't think about that. Maybe he should ask to take over biography. Only serious minded people would enter that section. Or maybe business or how-to, someplace where highly effective people congregate, not the flakes with wanderlust. Matt realized it wasn't worth it to bother making a change. He figured he wouldn't be working here too much longer. Something bigger and better was undoubtedly right around the corner.

Steve let out a loud yawn. "Late Saturday night?" Matt asked.

"More like an early Sunday morning."

"Didn't you just clock in?" The clock read 10:42. He made a stab at why Steve would need to get up early. "You go to church?"

"It takes me a while to start up in the morning."

"I had to be here at 7:30 to open, I had my alarm go off at 7:10, it took me eleven minutes to drive here, six minutes to walk from my parking spot and I was right on time."

"It's beautiful to be young, dumb, and full of cum. When you get around the sun a few more times, there's a lot more preparation to get through the day."

"Where I'm at right now is as good as it gets?"

"You're 24?"

"22."

"Late twenties are better. You still don't need much sleep after you drink and you know the way the world works a bit more. You know how to talk to women and maybe if you're lucky you're not dead broke."

Matt pushed his cart filled with books out of the swinging double doors and into the store. It was still pretty empty. As much as Matt hated to wake up so early, there was a fringe benefit to the morning shift, the day flew by. Before he knew it, it would be lunch. Then at 4 he'd be out of here. There would be plenty of time in the day. He could venture out and shoot some baskets, or head to the beach, or maybe he could find a place to watch the Niners game. They lost last week, but with Steve Young at quarterback, and Jerry Rice and Terrell Owens at wide receiver, they were bound to bounce back. Thinking about the 49ers gave Matt a pang of homesickness. He thought about watching games with his Dad and sister. He even harkened back to the couple times they went to Candlestick Park when his Dad marveled at Joe Montana and would say over and over with every one of his pass attempts, "That's how you throw a ball."

"Excuse me, can you tell me where the books on Hawaii are?'

Matt stood up from a crouching position to see what was a vision, a dream, a pretty girl talking to him. "Oh yeah, sure." He tried to walk smoothly to where the Pacific Island books were and he pointed right at them and then looked at her with her long, golden brown hair and cheekbones that sparkled with her smile. He did not want this to end right away. He tried to continue the conversation. "A lot of people like this publisher, if you're into off the beaten path type places. There aren't many pictures, but there's lots of words."

"Oh, thank you," she said as she flipped through it. "Have you been to Hawaii?"

"Yeah, I went there once with my family as a kid. My mom had a conference for work. We went to Pearl Harbor and the beaches were really, really nice. I'm from California so it wasn't far." Matt realized he was talking too much. He was losing her. He needed to ask her a question. "You have an accent. You're not from here either are you?"

"No, I'm from France." He was amazed by how charmingly she said, "France."

"I went there once."

"You travel quite a lot? California, here, Hawaii, France'

"Not as much as I'd like. But France was cool. I saw the Eiffel Tower, the Mona Lisa, Jim Morrison's grave." He wouldn't bring up that he went with his girlfriend, his ex-girlfriend, and they spent the whole weekend fucking and bickering. "You get to travel a lot too. Hawaii's far away from here."

"Yes, I know. I always wanted to go, so I think while I have my work visa I should take advantage. I think I will visit during your November holiday."

"Thanksgiving. Lucky, that will be awesome. I'm Matt." He stuck out his hand for her to shake.

"Your necklace has a different name."

Matt felt so silly that he put a fake name on his nametag at this moment. He thought it was charming and goofy to label himself as Tex. "It's a joke. My real name is Matt."

"Marylise," she said. She went in to kiss both his cheeks. This was heaven, Matt thought, or a foreign movie. Oh, please don't let this be a dream. "Nice to meet you."

As she walked away Matt was mentally kicking himself over and over. Ask for her phone number. Ask for it. He'd never done such a thing, but now would be the time, wouldn't it? As he built up the nerve, he walked out to the register only to see she was gone. He went back to the travel section and found some guidebooks of the American West lurking in Southeast Asia. He put them in their proper place.

Matt cheered himself up by realizing she knew where he worked. If she was interested, she'd come back. If she wasn't or had a significant other then he saved himself rejection. Matt couldn't believe it was already noon. Perhaps his luck had changed.

Matt walked up the stairs to clock out for lunch thinking nothing could ruin his day. Dan was leaning against the rail smirking at Matt. "I was watching you," Dan said. "I was pointing you out to all the other employees, telling everyone this is the slowest worker I've ever seen. I'd never seen anyone move so slowly. You're like a sloth conserving energy." Matt responded with a shrug. Nothing could ruin his day.

September 26, 1999
Rastaman Vibration

The rain came down. Not so hard that they felt the need to get back in the car, but frequently enough that they could not forget that they were standing in the rain. Matt looked out from the dock into the horizon. He squinted a bit and he thought he could see a small vessel rowing past the anchored sailboats into their direction. "Is that him?"

Jay took a moment before answering. "Yeah, I think so."

They braved the elements because a few days earlier Jay had met a man named Rasta Rick. Rick, as his name would suggest, was a Rastafarian. But contrary to stereotypes he was Caucasian. That did not stop Rasta Rick from growing long nappy dreadlocks and facial hair, sharing a love for reggae music, nor to having access to grade A marijuana. Jay shared one of Rasta Rick's joints and was instantly in love. He wanted more.

"More is a possibility." Rasta Rick told him. Once Jay could secure the funds, the cash, he was to give Rasta Rick a call on his beeper with the code "420". This is exactly what Jay had done. Now they were patiently waiting.

Jay explained to Matt the specifics he knew. Rasta Rick lived on a boat with his wife and child. They chartered back and forth between Jamaica and Florida, taking what was good from one land and transporting it to the other.

It was clear to Matt what Rasta Rick was smuggling to Miami. Matt was unsure what he would be taking to the islands. Jay took a stab, "I don't know. I think like shit from health food stores. He was talking a lot about royal jelly and how it's the honey made for queen bees."

Rasta Rick was getting closer. He pulled his boat up to the docks and tied it up. Jay gave him a hand to boost himself up to the mainland. Matt introduced himself to see if Rasta Rick introduced himself as Rasta Rick or just Rick. "Hi, I'm Matt."

"Jah bless," was all Rasta Rick responded with. He smelled strongly of the salts of the sea. His skin was tanned, but not enough to hide his ethnicity.

"Do you want to go into the car and drive?" Jay suggested.

They went into Matt's Peugeot and did just that. Matt turned on the ignition. The windshield wipers came on as did the radio. A football game was on. As Matt made a couple turns and hit a straightway he looked in his rearview mirror and saw Rasta Rick grab into the crotch of his pants and pull out a sturdy brick of weed. It had the stench normally associated with marijuana, but also, like its cultivator, of the sea. Jay picked it up paying notice to its red hairs and took a whiff. "I don't have a scale with me." Jay said. "How much is this supposed to be?"

"Give me two hundred."

Jay did as he was told. Matt was curious about their passenger. "What is it like living in a boat?"

"It's the only way to live, mon." After Rasta Rick counted the cash and put it in his crotch from whence the weed came, he added, "Soon it really will be the only way to live. Y2K is coming."

"Yeah, only a few months left to party like it's 1999."

"You better get all your partying done, mon. January one, it's all going to change."

Matt of course knew all about Y2K. He had read the countless articles and had the prerequisite late night paranoid conversations that at midnight of January 1, many computers would not be able to handle making sense of the year in its database going from '99 to '00. There were theories that programmers were shortsighted and malfunctions and catastrophes could be in the offering.

"It's going down, mon. We have become too dependent on technology. You read the bible?"

Jay was concerned about stowing away his purchase in his backpack as well as smoking a little portion of it, so Matt felt obliged to be the one to answer. "I've read parts of it."

"You know every time man gets too full of himself, God comes to humble. He does it with floods, with fire. This time Jah made us do it to ourselves. We have put microchips in everything. The hospitals, the traffic lights, the airplanes will fall from the sky. The only place that will be safe is the mighty ocean. I have myself prepared. We be away from all the trouble, the chaos that is going to come January the first."

"You think Jamaica will be okay?"

"Yeah mon, you go in the mountains, they have no computers. Those that have nothing now, will soon have everything."

Matt took a puff and passed it back saying the first thing that came to mind. "You grew up in Jamaica?"

"No mon, Connecticut."

"It must be quite a change."

"It is, but it is loving. It is the right place to be."

"And they're cool with you, there? I mean you know…"

Rasta Rick knew exactly what Matt meant. "Bob Marley's father is white. What is the color of the skin is not important. It is what is in here." Rasta Rick pounded his chest with his fist. He then began to cough violently. As Rasta Rick's composure came back he noticed a football game was on the radio. "Do you know, mon, the Patriots score?"

"No, this is the Dolphins game. I haven't really been paying attention to the scores." Matt drove them back towards the docks. They all shook hands and Rick bid farewell with a final "Jah Bless." Matt wiped up the windshield that had fogged up due to the condensation, not because of the smoke, and could see Rasta Rick untying his boat.

Jay couldn't contain his glee any longer. "I've got to get to a scale to prove it, but dude I think the guy gave me a thousand dollars worth of weed for like two hundred."

"I guess he figures pretty soon money won't be worth the printing it's papered on." Matt was pretty impressed with the way he mixed around that cliché. Jay didn't notice or at least he didn't comment upon it. For a second Matt thought Jay was offended that he was encroaching on his verbal turf. But then he noticed Jay was just smitten with the weed he had just purchased. Matt asked, "You think there's any truth to what he was saying? The whole Y2K thing?"

"For sure, man. This, all of this, none of it is sustainable."

October 1, 1999
Payments Due

Matt wrote out the check for his portion of the rent. He knocked on the building manager's door the other day to ask who he should make the check out to. She was a little perturbed that this was the first time she had met Matt. "People keep moving in and out. It's not right."

"I'm sorry. I didn't know the procedure."

"Sure, you didn't." Matt stood there for a second not sure what he should say. "It's fine. It's fine. I'll make up a new lease for the unit." She went back in and gave him a stapled pile of papers. "Sign it and give it back to me with the rent."

Matt filled it out along with the check. He did not see where John might have left his share of the rent, so he walked to his bedroom door and tapped it lightly. There was no answer. Matt banged louder. Still nothing. "John?" he whispered and then yelled.

Matt nudged open the door. It was the first time he had entered John's part of the apartment. The blinds were closed tighter than Matt would have imagined possible. On their drive to the beach the other day, their first time together outside the apartment, John had issued as an anecdote, but also as kind of a warning that his previous roommate used to snoop around his room.

"How could you tell?" Matt asked. "Were things missing?"

"No, but I place things strategically, if anyone enters I know."

Matt realized this was all bluster with a little bit of nonsense thrown in. There was not much in the room. There was a mattress with sheets laid flatly on the carpet. Next to that was an empty cardboard box with a lamp and alarm clock flashing the wrong time atop it. There were no photos, no books, nor personal mementos laying anywhere. There was one drawing taped on to the wall. It took Matt a moment to decipher it was a handcrafted diagram of their apartment's floor plan. Matt then was surprised to learn, John had his own bathroom. It made sense since there were no strange toothbrushes in his bathroom, but this was the first he was aware of it.

Matt looked into the small bathroom. At first he was surprised it was cleaner than his, but then he looked into the toilet. Matt flushed it. He couldn't help himself. Then he realized perhaps that mess was the way John knew someone had entered his domain?

As the green water returned to fill up the toilet bowl, Matt realized that was not shit, it was algae. In his sheltered life, Matt had no idea such a thing was possible, that your toilet water could turn into such a deep shade of green. He quickly fled John's part of the apartment. He left a note for John that he taped on his door. "Please leave your rent on the kitchen table."

Matt hoped John had the funds to pay the rent. Creditors called every night at 6 p.m. almost like clockwork looking to speak to him. One night when Jay stayed over they had some fun with the phone call.

"Is this John Randall Suarez?"

"Of course." Jay said as he put the bill collector on speaker phone. "What time will you come make sweet love to me, my dear?"

"Sir, I'm calling on behalf of Sally Mae in reference to your delinquent loan payments."

"No, you do not have to worry about paying me to be delinquent. I will bring out the handcuffs and chains free of charge. For a lady as beautiful as you I should be the one that is paying."

"Sir, this is not a laughing matter." She said as she was holding back laughter just as much as Matt was.

"You are correct. This is not a matter of laughter. This is a matter of screams and moans and ecstasy."

It took the woman on the phone a second to figure out what she was to do next. "Look, John I'm here to call about your student loans…"

"John?"

"Yes, you said you were John Suarez."

"Ah, I misheard you. I thought you asked for Don Morris. Who is this scoundrel, John Suarez? Is he my rival for your hand?"

"You are not John Suarez?"

"No, you scandalous tease. You arouse me with your voice and then you tell me you are looking for someone else? How dare you? How dare---" for the first time in human history a debt collector hung up on the person they were calling.

Every 6:00 after that when Matt heard the phone ring he was tempted to try something as mischievous. But there was no audience and he felt a little bad for John. When they made it to the beach the day before as the waves hit the white sand John turned to him and said, "I forgot how beautiful three dimensions can be."

October 2, 1999
Bliss and Shit

Matt had given up on her. It had been two weeks since he had seen her. So when Marylise walked up to the information booth where he was stationed with her smile and French accent to say "Hello," Matt's words were somehow deeply immersed in his throat.

Finally, he managed a "hi." He wanted to say "bon jour" but knew he would foul that up terribly. "How are you doing? Can I help you find any books or music?" He wanted to kill himself. He went into corporate speak, how the managers told him to address customers.

"Yes, I would like a new book to read."

"Cool. Come with me." He led her up the stairs. "I guess I'm being a little presumptuous. I don't think we have too many books in French, we have a lot in Spanish. Are books in English fine?"

"Of course. Is my English that bad?"

"No, it's really good. But it's just bad enough to be charming." It came out so smoothly in Matt's mind before he spoke it, but by her silence he did not think it was taken as well as he hoped. "Do you want fiction or non-fiction?"

"Fiction."

"Happy or sad?"

"A combination of both."

He had some ideas, but he wanted it to be perfect. "Have you ever read *Catcher in the Rye* by J.D. Salinger."

"No, I heard of it. It's very famous."

'Okay, this is even better." He handed her a paperback copy of *Nine Stories* by J.D. Salinger. He had just read it and was moved by the humor and ennui.

She looked it over very carefully. He really hoped she liked it. "This looks nice. Merci. I'm glad you are here. I came on Sunday and did not see you. I thought you moved back to California?"

Now he was a jellyfish. She came to see him not once, but twice? "They give me Sundays off. I get one part of the weekend free now."

"How nice."

He had no idea how to do this. He had never done it, but he would try anyway. "Could I have your phone number? You know, then you could tell me how you like the book. Then you won't have to worry about hunting me down, you'd know my work schedule ahead of time."

"Of course," she said allowing a dignified end to his rambling awkwardness. He hunted down a pen and a scrap of paper and wrote her numbers down, all seven of them and put it in a special spot in his wallet. She kissed both of his cheeks good-bye and it was like gravity no longer existed. How was such a thing even possible? There was someone in the world, someone amazing who seemed interested in him. It made him glad for once to be alive and had him thinking about a concept he had been pondering a lot, how every previous moment in the history of humanity, hell, in the history of the universe, had led to right now.

As the glories of being alive filled Matt's head, mere hours later there was already someone willing to bring him back to reality. "Matt, I need you to go to the bathroom---"

"I already took my second break."

His manager Dan clarified what he meant. "No, I need you to clean up a mess in there."

"Don't we have janitors to do that?"

"They don't come until the store closes and this needs to be taken care of now."

Matt was in too positive a state of mind to question any further. He skipped two steps at a time to go upstairs to the men's room. He swung open the door and saw in the sole urinal the mess that needed cleaning up. Before he felt the need to retch, he almost laughed. Someone had taken a sloppy shit in the urinal. Drops of it were on the tile floor, but a majority of it stagnated in the porcelain pouch meant for urine

He was almost laughing at the scenario when he walked out of the bathroom. Dan was there though to tell him, "I'm having someone bring up cleaning supplies."

"Are you serious? I'm not touching that."

"I am serious and we have gloves so you don't have to touch it."

For a moment Matt had it in his head that it was Dan who had created that bathroom foulness. He had the image of his massive body squatting over the urinal. "That isn't my job."

"Your job is to do what I tell you.'

"Well, you can fire me then." Matt meant it. He didn't need this or any material possession. He could subsist on the good feelings Marylise brought out in him. For a second he thought that was what he would be forced to do.

But Dan's stare down ended with him rolling his eyes and sighing, "Fine, I'll get someone else."

Matt went back to the information booth. He took a couple phone calls. He directed a customer to the CD with the song "Genie in a Bottle" on it. Throughout Matt kind of kept his eye upstairs to see who was going to be responsible for the bathroom.

Eventually he spied Steve pushing open the door and walking out as fast as his unbending knees would take him.

Matt couldn't help but to ask him, "They didn't make you clean out the bathroom, did they?"

"Fuck you, Matt." Steve said so all the customers could hear as he limped out of the store.

Matt was kind of dumbfounded. He'd never been cursed out in such a public setting. He saw Dan grinning and looked for guidance toward the situation from his superior. "Did he just quit?"

"No. He went home to change his clothes." Matt tried to imagine what situation during cleaning that could cause any of that slop to get on his clothes. "Some people have pride in their work ethic."

Matt didn't defend himself. He didn't make the mess, all he did was refuse to clean it. Dan could have cleaned it himself, but still Matt felt a deep dosage of shame when just moments before he thought nothing could bring him back to Earth.

October 8, 1999
The Big Date

"I'm really sorry for the other day." Matt said to Steve in the cage. It was the first time they had worked together since Saturday and Matt had felt awful throughout.

"For what?" Steve said as he inserted CD's into their theftproof plastic security cases.

"Saturday when you had to clean the bathroom…"

"You did that? Why the fuck did you shit in the urinal?"

"No. No. God no. Dan told me to clean it before you."

"And you told him to fuck off?"

"No, I mean I told him he could fire me. I wasn't going to do it."

Steve chuckled. "God, I must be getting old. It didn't even cross my mind to say no. Good for you, no apology needed." Steve said with a yawn which gave Matt an idea on how he could rectify the situation.

"I know you hate these early morning shifts, if you ever want to trade a later shift with me just ask."

"That's okay. I was just up late watching the Mets. They're playing west coast times in the playoffs against a shitty Arizona team."

Matt didn't even know the playoffs started. He figured that meant neither of his teams made it to the postseason. Just to make sure he asked, "The Giants or the A's aren't still playing, are they?"

"No they both sucked this year. I forgot, you're a California kid."

"Yeah, my dad likes the Giants. When the A's were good that was my team."

"Jose Canseco, Miami's finest. I remember that one. It's funny no other sport gets me, but whoever wins the World Series, even if it's the fucking Yankees I start crying. I see that catcher run to the pitcher and hug and they all pile on to each other and it gets me. That's fucking happiness. That's fucking fulfillment."

"I cry every time I watch *Field of Dreams*." Matt said. That was a baseball movie after all.

"Yeah, that's a fucking tearjerker."

"You used to play baseball?"

"No, when I was a kid I did, but I just love watching the sport especially the Mets when they don't piss off. I played hockey." Then without warning Steve pulled his teeth away from his gums to reveal the whole top set were fakes.

"What the fuck?" Matt couldn't help but to scream. "You lost all those teeth playing hockey?"

"A lot of them. Others I lost, I don't want to get into how I lost them. That's why I told you your late twenties can be the best time of your life if you don't do anything stupid. I did stupid things." Then for emphasis Steve took his teeth out again.

Matt knew that second time was to mess with him after his scaredy cat reaction, but he couldn't man up and remain stoic. That was one of his recurring nightmares, he'd lose his teeth in a variety of ways. One would come out while he was eating, then he'd pull at some other teeth and they'd fall out too. Until that moment he never realized that was one of his true phobias during waking hours. It was hard for him to even look at Steve any more. He now saw him as a creature that was in the process of decomposing.

Matt wouldn't let the thought of our mortality, get him too down. Tonight, was the night. Marylise was going to meet him when his shift ended at seven. The first part of his day went so slow, but as afternoon turned into evening time sped up much too fast.

Nerves floated around his stomach. Did he not dress up enough for the occasion? Matt had lately been a chatterbox to his co-workers. He expressed every little inconvenience, frustration with a rude customer, and funny encounter with whoever was in the break room or on the floor with him. But he kept the existence of this date quiet. Any triumph or failure that arose this evening would be his and his alone.

He smiled as he realized how long it had been since he had thought about Erin. Her rejection of him had weighed heavily ever since he left, but now was forgotten. He was so proud of himself. All he needed was to substitute one obsession for another.

After clocking out and walking downstairs he didn't see Marylise anywhere and began to panic. Was there a misunderstanding on their phone call? She said she would meet him at the store at seven, but they never stated where in the store. He went out toward the entrance and then he saw her, she wore a black dress and she smiled at him. She kissed both his cheeks. "Right on time," she said.

He felt awful that he was not as pretty as her. He did not take as good a care of any part of his being as she did of her sandy brown hair. He held the door open for her even though he was uncertain where they should go. He was not sure what was expected of him so he suggested what he believed people on dates were supposed to do. "Would you like to see a movie?"

"Yes," she said. They walked to the theater. He asked her about her day and she recounted. They looked at the movie times and tried to make sense of what to see based on titles and posters. They settled on *American Beauty*, but they had an hour until it was playing. "Should we eat dinner?" she suggested.

"What a great idea." He really and truly thought that was brilliant. He had forgotten to eat with all his anxiety. Most of the restaurants in Coconut Grove always seemed overpriced and depressing to eat at alone, but now he was with someone he would throw every dime into a wishing well to be around. He picked the first restaurant he saw with sidewalk tables and told her, 'This place is great."

He looked at the menu. Everything was over $20. He panicked for a second, then the waiter came trying to push wine on them. She ordered a glass of some sort and he asked for the same. "I don't know anything about wine. You're going to have to tell me if it's good or not."

"You are funny," she said. He thanked her even though he didn't mean to be funny. She added, "I started the book you suggested."

"Do you like it?"

"It's interesting. The Perfect Day for Bananas."

"Bananafish."

"Yes. What are those? Bananafish?"

"I had a teacher in college who said they weren't fish. Seymore Glass was showing the little girl... his you know... his penis."

"Oh. That's terrible. I don't know if I like the story then."

"Yeah, I didn't like that interpretation either. It kind of ruins it. I like to think it's about how there's so much mystery in the world, if you just take the time to look at it with a child's eyes. But society always beats it out of you when you grow up."

"I didn't like that he killed himself."

"No, there's not much to like about suicide. I used to be suicidal." Why the fuck did he just tell her that? He wanted to get up and literally kick himself. That's the tiniest amount of punishment he felt he deserved. Is he trying to sabotage himself? He's supposed to charm her, not reveal the darkness in his soul that he constantly battled. But her response was just to smile and nod and he realized the volume of their outdoor seating and the language barrier might have saved him.

The waiter then brought the wine. "A votre sante is how we cheer in French." She told him.

"In America we say cheers to the white rabbit."

"Really?"

"No. That's something me and my sister used to say when kids. We'd bang our water glasses and say cheers to the white rabbit."

"Cheers to the white rabbit," she said and they clinked glasses. "You are close with your sister?"

"Sometimes. She's in college in California. We talk on the phone a little and send each other e-mails. Do you have brothers or sisters?"

"Yes, my older brother is in France."

"Uh, oh."

"Why uh, oh?"

"An older brother, would he try to beat me up if he knew I was taking you on a date?"

"No, he'd be happy I was spending time with somebody nice."

Somebody nice. Matt liked that. He was nice, at least to her. If they came across a puddle, he would without a moment's hesitation lay down his coat for her to walk upon. Their dinner came, as did more conversation. She ate very slowly, and for that Matt was very grateful. He was hopeful the meal would never end. It was the happiest dinner he had in months, maybe years, but he feared payment. He had lost count on her second glass of wine of what he owed.

When the bill came in a black leather book, Marylise reached for it. He almost let her take it, but he knew that would be disaster. He was grateful that after the tip he still had $5 to last him for the weekend. Lady luck continued to smile on him when they walked over to the theater box office to see not only *American Beauty* was sold out, but so was every other movie they were halfway interested in. "Maybe it's a good thing," he said in hopes of seeming smooth. "I'd rather look and listen to you than any movie star."

They walked around the stores and bars. The cars on Grand Avenue were at a standstill and for once Matt felt like he was part of something. Some grand human experiment where billions of humans were spread out all around the world and we had to do our best to find our kindred spirits. And goddamn he'd done it. He had to leave California and she had to come all the way from France, but here they were together under the Florida moon sitting on the bleachers of Peacock Park talking about their separate histories.

Their conversation hit a stop. He looked at her and she at him. This was it. This was the moment all those romantic comedies said was when he should act. "Can I kiss you?" he asked.

She blushed. "No."

That kind of took him for a loop. Why did he ask, why didn't he just kiss her? "I'd really like to," was all he could muster.

"I am not ready," she said.

"Okay. I respect that. I'm patient. Just so you know I'm ready when you're ready."

Soon after she said it was getting late. He walked her back to her car. She kissed him on both his cheeks. "I had a wonderful time. Thank you for dinner."

"It was awesome. Maybe we can do it again tomorrow?" he said without remembering that he had no money. But he did realize aloud. "I close tomorrow though so I couldn't hang out until midnight."

"That is too late," she said before entering the car. "Call me and we will figure it out." As she pulled out of the parking spot and drove down the street he wanted to call her right then.

October 12, 1999
The Dinner Party

Jay was simultaneously impressed by his friend's story about Marylise and also incredibly disappointed. "You asked her if you could kiss her? You asked her?"

"I know. I know."

Jay continued as though Matt didn't know. "There's no romance in that. You've got to act like you can't help yourself, that the world's forces are leading you together. You don't want to be cold and calculating, you want to seem passionate. Plus, like everything in life, it's always better to ask for forgiveness than permission."

Jay was preaching to the choir. Matt knew he royally screwed things up. But Marylise gave him another shot. Her friend was in town from France for the week. Matt suggested they all come over for dinner. He would cook them his specialty, vegetable curry. She said she would bring the red wine and chocolate cake. Matt said he also had a friend who could make the dinner a foursome.

Enter Jay who was ever so happy to meet a mysterious French woman. His skin had tanned and he was filled with adventurous stories to impress her. Since Matt had last seen Jay he went with Rasta Rick on a smuggling trip to Jamaica.

With the vegetables and rice simmering Matt decided to take a shower. It wasn't just that he wanted to be clean, he wanted to get his thoughts in order. He was nervous again, but before panic could set in, Jay ordered him to use a bottle of conditioner acquired in Jamaica. "It will make you smell tropical."

Matt entered his private chamber and turned on the faucet. Hot drips spiked his skin and he dreaded all the things that could go wrong. He told Jay not to make any mention of Erin. He also told him not to discuss any illegal activities he took part in. What if John showed up? He never came home at this time, but he could make the whole thing awkward. Matt regretted smoking pot earlier.

He turned off the water and toweled off. He noticed as he buttoned up his shirt that the conditioner did smell tropical, like a coconut. He exited the shower with perfect timing. Not only was the food ready, but Marylise was at the door with her friend Marie. Introductions were made and cheeks were kissed. Matt could tell Marie was a little plump for Jay's taste, but God bless his friend for acting all kinds of interested.

Marylise handed Matt a bottle of wine and the chocolate cake. She was looking beautiful, beautiful. Every time he looked at her a smile came to his face. He was already planning a honeymoon, but then she broke his heart. "Is that a new style?"

Matt looked down at his shirt. He had buttoned it all wrong. One side of the shirt was closer to his chin than the other. He couldn't even look at her. Here she was all dressed up in a tight ponytail and clean clothes and he was unable to even put on his shirt correctly.

They drank the good bottle first. They were sufficiently buzzed, so the three dollar bottle Jay bought didn't taste so bad until they reached the chalky sediment at the bottle of the cup. Everyone mingled but Matt stayed quiet. He hung on every one of Marylise's words, even the one's Jay mocked later in his faux French accent. "I started rollerblading. I should take classes. I know how to go, but I do not know how to brake and that is very dangerous."

After cake everyone moved into the living room. Matt suggested to Marylise, "Do you want to check out my balcony?" They stepped outside and tried to find stars. The weed and wine really limbered up his conversational skills. He began to tell her of the time he saw a UFO. She spoke of how her friend was already driving her crazy and was unsure how their weekend trip to Key West would go. He described a beach where he would like to one day take her. She told him she was glad to meet someone so friendly.

He went in to kiss her. Better forgiveness than permission. She let him taste the wine on her lips and then said, "No."

"I'm sorry. I know you're much too good for me. I'm broke and I can't put on my shirt and---"

"No, I like you. My last boyfriend he was rich, but he would ignore me. You, you are different. You don't take anything seriously."

"That's just the side I show you."

"That's the side I like." She kept smiling as she said her next words, "My father died two years ago."

"I'm sorry."

"My family says I'm running away from it. I came to America right afterwards. First Kansas and then here and the reason that it is bad is right before my father died, I caught him with another woman than my mother." She said it without shedding a tear from her pale eyes. "I'm not ready to trust anyone."

"Even me?" He asked which made her smile a little sadder.

"Let's go inside," she said, grabbing him by the hand.

Opening the sliding glass door revealed what was going on inside. Jay and Marie had their tongues inside each other's mouths. Matt could swear he saw Jay's hand up her shirt, but they quickly separated when two became four. Marylise spoke some words in French. Marie ran up to her and responded in the same mysterious language. Marylise translated. "Marie is going to stay."

It was apparent that Marylise was not willing to. "I'll walk you out." Matt told her. He grabbed the pan that held the remnants of her chocolate cake.

They walked down the stairs on to the street. "I'm glad you came. I like getting to know you. I'm sorry that your friend is…"

"It's good. She's getting on my how do you say, my hair."

Matt didn't correct her. He understood what she meant. "I hope you have a good time on your trip with her this weekend and maybe when you get back…" Marylise began talking to herself in French. The only words he could understand were "Marie" and "merde." She kissed both of his cheeks and said "merci" and drove off.

Matt watched as her car made a left away from his vantage point. He walked back up the stairs. Jay and Marie were no longer in his living room. Matt was still a little drunk so he didn't quite put two and two together until he reached for his doorknob and it was locked. Then he noticed a dirty sock had been placed on the doorknob and music, the soundtrack from *Trainspotting* played amidst giggles.

Matt didn't care. Once he had an injury, it didn't matter how many insults were piled on. He collapsed on the couch and just as he was about to fall asleep he heard the front door open. For a second he thought it was Marylise. She would throw herself into his arms and he would tell her everything would be okay.

But instead it was his roommate, John. He walked in and surveyed the empty glasses and plates on the table. "You had a party?"

"Yeah, it kind of died early." Matt had to tell his frustrations to someone. "I'm in love with a girl. All I do is I think about her. When I'm around her everything feels good, but she told me she just wanted to be my friend, and like an idiot I told her okay, fine."

John fished around his collection of videotapes that Matt piled neatly on the ground in hope of neatening up the place for the French girls. "It's nice to have friends."

"No, friends suck." Matt corrected him.

"I once loved a girl." John told him as he chose a tape to insert into the VCR. But as John went into the depths of his heartbreak and his loss Matt had already fallen asleep.

October 15, 1999
A Trip to the Movies

"I'm sorry. I changed your sheets and everything." Jay waited in the store, patiently flipping through Salvador Dali coffee table art books, until his friend ended work. As they went outside, Matt continued to be quiet. Jay realized Matt wasn't ignoring him due to an attempt to seem professional in his work environment. It was obvious Matt was mad at him. "If I had my own place I would have done the same favor for you."

"When are you getting your own place?'

"What is it? You're pissed I got some and you didn't?" Yes, that was it, but Matt would never acknowledge such a thing. But he did not need to, as Jay had accepted this explanation for his friend's demeanor. "You shouldn't set your standards so high. You're always going for these pretty girls."

"She is pretty, isn't she?"

"Yeah, she's fucking beautiful, so she's going to be a pain in the ass. It's going to take work and luck and skill because every time she leaves her house she has half a dozen guys whistling and offering to hold the door open for her."

"Marie is pretty too."

"She's hundreds of times prettier than my right hand. And she's only in town for a week, those are the girls you should go for. She wants adventure and romance on her vacation. You had to pick the one French girl who lives here. It's okay. You need to sign up for my class on seduction. Or you can watch the tv show I have. The theme song is, 'if you want to be happy for the rest of your life get yourself an ugly wife.'"

Matt didn't want to go into this any further. "Do you want to see a movie? I kind of want to check out that new Brad Pitt movie –it had a Pixies song in the preview."

"We could do that." Jay said as he sat down on a bus stop bench. "Or we could do this?"

Matt sat down to see what Jay was cupping in his hand. It was a clear plastic little baggie that contained perforated pieces of white blotter paper. "Acid?"

"Yeah, Rasta Rick knows a chemist who lives in Jamaica. He says it's awesome and pure. Wanna?"

"Maybe, let's do it after the movie. I really want to see it."

"Let's do both. We'll drop it now. It takes a while for it to kick in, by the time the movie is over we'll be peaking."

Without thinking it over more, Matt took a square and placed it on his tongue. Jay smiled and did the same. Maybe it was powerful LSD or maybe it was psychosomatic, but from the moment it touched him, Matt could feel the drug beginning to affect him.

They walked over to the movie theater box office and bought two tickets for the *Fight Club* screening that started five minutes earlier. They took their seats in the dark room in a middle row where neither of them had to sit immediately next to someone else.

After sitting through a couple previews, the movie began. It started with throbbing electronic music over the opening credits simulating the fast paced ride through the neurons of a brain. Matt gasped. This was obviously a coincidence, but this also was a real time demonstration of the acid coursing into his own brain. Matt knew that was how the drug worked, it made everything seem connected. The smallest, least significant event, could be a metaphor for anything else occurring in your life. But this viewing experience was beyond any happenstance, this was fate.

Almost from the start Matt could not help but to feel this movie was made especially for him. Everything from Ed Norton's abject loneliness as the movie's nameless protagonist, to his sense of humor despite hopelessness, to his explanation on why people live only to buy, buy, buy—it all connected. Matt looked over to Jay and did not need to say anything. Matt simply pointed at the screen in awe and Jay responded with his jaw agape, "I know, right!"

There was a love interest in Marla, played by a goth Helena Bonham Carter, who was as lost and disturbed as the protagonist. But the true love interest was Tyler Durden played by a manic Brad Pitt. All machismo and charisma Tyler Durden convinced the narrator that there is a reason to live and that is to feel something, anything even if it is just pain. So, they start Fight Club, a club where bare-chested men brawl. But soon that is not enough. Now that these men felt fixed they wanted to fix the world from all its flaws and hypocrisies and materialism. They begin one anarchic act after another with plenty of witty lines interspersed between moments of poignancy. When Marla turns to the narrator to say "I haven't been fucked like that since grade school." Matt lost it before he felt self-conscious over whether he seemed like a creep for laughing.

Then came the twist. In retrospect it was obvious, but when it revealed, Matt felt stunned. Tyler Durden was the narrator and the narrator was Tyler Durden. That moment seemed so true. We all have two sides. The reserved face we put on for society and the true self that is wild and alive that we constrain so we can fit in. Matt looked over at Jay and wondered for a moment if they too were in fact the same person. The id and the superego. Had anyone actually seen the pair together at the same time?

The movie ended with chaos and violence with the narrator desperately trying to stop Tyler Durden's plot to blow up credit card companies so that all debt could disappear. Marla is brought in and gasps when she sees the narrator shot himself in the face to kill the wild aspect of himself. She's stunned by his self-inflicted damages, but she takes him by the hand as the world is blowing up around them and the Pixies song, "Where is my Mind" gets louder and louder, when the narrator says, "You met me at a very strange time in my life" immediately before the credits. Matt couldn't help himself but to get up and clap. He was the only person to do this, not even Jay joined in, but he didn't care. This was a masterpiece even more than that it was truth and it helped him see he had done Erin wrong.

None of us are perfect in this goddamned corrupt world. We all have our scars, but when you find that kindred spirit you have to hold on to it and fight for it for all its worth or else this world will kill you. "Holy shit." Matt kept saying as they exited the theater.

"That was fucking incredible," was all Jay said until he added, "I've got to use the bathroom."

Matt followed him into the lobby and it was then that he felt fully aware of the power of what he had ingested. Everyone looked so fucking weird. It wasn't like they looked like cartoon characters, it was more they looked like lazy slabs of flesh waiting in line to buy junk food and ready to turn their minds off for two hours of diversions uncaring about any revolution that should be going on. Matt quickly felt depressed and also a little freaked out. As soon as he made eye contact with Jay exiting from the bathroom, Matt nearly sprinted down the stairs to get the hell out of there. Jay caught up to him and wanted to discuss the movie, but Matt kept silent not wanting to be around any of these people. When they walked downhill toward Peacock Park Matt finally felt comfortable to join in on a conversation. "This is some strong shit."

"Yeah."

"Do you think the movie was that good or do you think LSD just makes any movie that much better?"

Jay said he thought they just got lucky. "The only other time I dropped and watched a movie we went to see *Toy Story*. It wasn't life changing like that. Afterward I just remembered we all hopped in the back of a pick-up truck and I felt like the toys wiggling around not in control of where I was going. It was kind of fun though."

"I feel like when this stuff wears down I'll need to see the movie again. It was like telling the story of my life."

"That was the movie of our generation. That and Radiohead. I don't know how they fucking got it made. You wouldn't think the corporations would let them tell us how they're manipulating us to be numb unfeeling zombies spending all our lives working so we could buy things we don't even fucking need. We should be alive always trying to feel something." Jay jumped up from the bleachers and started putting up his dukes. "Come on, let's do it. Let's fight."

"No way."

"Come on, when's the last time you punched someone?"

"When we got jumped last month and you got your tooth chipped."

"Oh yeah. That fucking sucked. I still don't think my jaw feels completely right."

"You really think Radiohead is that good?"

"Man, haven't you heard *OK Computer*?" Jay began digging through his backpack. It was filled with a hundred souvenirs of a vagabond lifestyle. Finally, out came a walkman with a couple cassettes. He figured out which one was appropriate and gave one head phone to Matt and kept the other for himself.

Matt was taken to another world from the opening guitar riff. Even though his right ear could hear the passing traffic he was transported to alien landscapes and a dystopia founded by the encroachment of technology. After several songs a black man with a limp walked up and asked, "Yo, you fellas want to buy some weed?"

Jay jumped off the bleachers and asked the traveling merchant, "Why does everything have to be a transaction? Why can't you---"

Matt took advantage of Jay getting up to put the other headphone in his ear immersing himself completely into the music. He saw the stranger walk away as Jay kept preaching toward him. Matt heard a song, it was less a song and more a monologue from an automated voice speaking of all the routines a modern man goes through. It ended with "Fitter healthier and more productive/ a pig in a cage on antibiotics."

Not much later the tape began slowing and slowing until Matt realized the batteries had died. "It's hella good, right?" Jay asked.

"Yeah, your batteries are done."

"Soon, they'll all be done." Jay said trying to suffuse meaning out of every one of his words and gestures. "What we're doing to the world is unsustainable."

"I remember," Matt said, "when I was a kid I heard the sun was going to explode in a billion years and I couldn't sleep at night with the idea that it was all going to end."

"It's going to happen much sooner than that the way we treat this world. It's all going to end."

"Of course, we're all going to die. Death is the end of the world for each of us."

"No, but I mean as a species we're going to die. Unless we might be smarter than we think. Maybe the Y2K is going to save us all.

Humans knew in the back of their minds all these computers, all these oil dependent toys were going to end us, so they hit a reset button. On January 1, 2000 the automated world will end. It will suck at first, but maybe we can build something better. A civilization that can last until the sun burns us all out."

"You spent too much time on that boat with Rasta Rick."

"I did, but he's right, man. We've got to prepare. You can't just pretend it's not going to happen.'

Matt started thinking how we all live our lives doing our best to pretend it will never end. It's about the here and now and right this moment. And right now he was thirsty so they began walking back to Cocowalk where there was a water fountain. Matt tried not to stare too hard at any of the people, not the women in their tight clothing or the men with the expensive drinks in their hands. Then he heard his name. Matt tried to ignore it until he could not.

It was his co-workers. Oceana, Diego, and Mayra. He couldn't quite follow what they were saying. It took all his will power not to freak out at the people walking around and the fluorescent lighting making everything look so weird. "A few friends are coming over to my place if you want to join?" one of them asked. Jay answered yes for the both of them. As they walked to the car Matt let his friend know, "Don't let them know we're on acid." Jay agreed to keep it confidential. They hopped in the backseat of Oceania's car and were taken to a house that seemed much too large for someone their age to live at alone. It was explained it was Mayra's aunt's and she could live there until the property was sold.

The house was large and empty without a single piece of furniture in the living room. Beers were offered out of the not as empty fridge and were taken out back where a swimming pool waited for them in all its wetness. Matt did not need to be asked twice if he wanted to swim. While he made a conscious decision not to tell his co-workers he was tripping, he felt like he had no need to hide his physical self from them. He stripped down to his boxers and dove in. He held his breath as long as he could before floating up and letting the water support him. He looked up at the clouds moving in the dark sky and he thought about his place in the universe. He always figured he was important. That there was some significance to his existence, but maybe he was just a cloud floating in the sky, that only those clouds that he happened to pass by would be aware of.

Matt began thinking of the movie *Fight Club* again. Was there a reason why he saw it on this night of all nights? Maybe Matt could have some historical significance? Maybe like the movie's narrator he needed to start a revolution. He pulled himself out of the pool and for the first time noticed a boat had been parked in the backyard. Jay was on top of it with Mayra asking her all kinds of questions, like who it belonged to and when was the last time it was used. Matt started drying himself by brushing the water off his body with his hands.

Diego and Oceana were playing a guitar and bongo drums. Oceana yelled out to Matt, "You can change in the house."

Matt grabbed his clothes and did just that. As he walked inside to the full blast of air conditioning he took off his boxers and hung it from a shower rod. He took a good look at himself. This is it. This is who you are. He put on his clothes sans underwear and was about to head outside when he noticed a computer. He decided there was something he needed to do. He sat down and logged into his e-mail account. It took a while for the page to load, but once it did he typed an e-mail to Erin that cackled with electricity. He wrote with such eloquence and passion that he wondered if he always took LSD if he could be the J.D. Salinger of the 21st century. When he finished the message with "Love, Matt" he knew it was not perfect. Whereas usually Matt would proofread an e-mail for grammatical errors, he knew that would just dilute his message of forgiveness and hope, and so he hit send.

Matt stepped away from the computer when the screen read "your message has been sent." He logged out and stepped outside to see Mayra playing a blues riff on the guitar and Jay making up words on the spot. "Communism party!" "Communism party!" Jay kept repeating over and over again.

Matt was on the same wavelength and joined in "Communism Party! Communism Party!"

Jay smiled that he had someone else singing along. Matt could envision this party of communists. All wearing sunglasses and black berets. Maybe a couple dashikis thrown in? Matt envisioned it so well he even threw in another line "eat your borscht it's hearty."

"The Communism Party!"

"The Communism Party!"

Matt was so excited about the song and about everything else he said, "I think I can do a backflip."

Oceana grabbed Matt by the arm. "You've got me scared."

"Don't worry," he told her, "I won't do it. But I could."

October 16, 1999
The Comedown

Matt woke up to morning showers. He'd slept on the pool furniture which was comfortable enough. The gray clouds that protected him from the sun were not so kind when dealing with the rain. When he saw the time though he was grateful for the weather. He had to be at work in thirty minutes. He left his car by the store so he wouldn't even have time to swing home and change. With the drug worn off he no longer had the urge to necessarily start a revolution, but with his underwear still wet he figured he would be acting rebellious enough by entering society without any protection from his zipper.

Matt looked around for Jay and found him sleeping inside the cabin of the boat. "I'm leaving for work," he told him. Jay just waved his arm at him. Matt exited through the house seeing no signs of life so he kept walking until outside. He was very low on energy. The night before had used up all his reserves. He came to the same conclusion he reached every time he used a psychedelic in that he should be able to create these thoughts, feelings, and ideas on his own without the dependence of any foreign substance.

The day was unspectacular. When Mayra and Diego both checked in they mocked him with a little rendition of "Communism Party." The only other moment of note was when he worked the cash register and heard a man who was buying a get rich quick book talk to his friend about how he saw the movie *Fight Club* and that it was terrible. Matt couldn't muster up the energy to correct him.

When he clocked out he saw his car parked under the shade of a tree for a day and a half had been showered in white bird droppings. That did not affect him. Not much he figured would stop him from a heavy date with his pillow. He would make a proper visit to dreamland and maybe sleep through Sunday as well.

But as he pulled his still damp boxer shorts out of his pocket he had to check the answering machine that was flashing its red light, indicating three messages. The first two were creditors looking for John.

The third grabbed his attention. "Hi, Matt." It was Erin. "I got your e-mail. It wasn't making a whole lot of sense. I guess you're doing what you're doing. Call me when you get a chance. I just want to make sure everything is all right."

He called. He knew the number by heart. It used to be his, the number and coincidentally also his heart. "Hello?" By some miracle Erin picked up on the first ring.

"Hi Erin, it's me. It's Matt."

"I know who 'me' is."

"I'm glad one of us does." She didn't laugh even though Matt thought that was kind of witty. "So, I wasn't making much sense last night? I thought it was the best piece of writing I'd done since I left you a note about your mom calling."

She chuckled at that one. "I don't know, I've been reading your comic book columns in your paper. Your review on *Eightball* almost made me stop at the comic book shop. But yeah, that e-mail was kind of weird. I couldn't tell if it was a mission statement for yourself or some kind of weird suicide note."

"It was a little of both, I guess. It really didn't make sense? I thought I was being crystal clear.'

"I understood you liked the movie *Fight Club* and that you wanted to start a revolution "

"Didn't I also say that I loved you and that we should do what it takes so that we can be together?" She didn't say anything about that. "That's what I meant to write anyway. I did acid last night."

"Yeah, I figured it was something like that."

"But I meant every word I wrote."

"I know you did. You always do, unless you don't." There was silence for a while. "I'll let you go. You sound tired."

"Yeah, I had to work today. I don't think I got much sleep last night. You can come join me in my bed or at least your voice can. I'll bring the phone—"

"No, I should go. I just wanted to make sure you were alright."

"I am."

"Okay, well then take care."

She hung up. Matt was tired, dirty. He was going to drop it, but something about her voice reminded him of the past. He called her back. "Erin, is everything okay?"

"Yeah," she said.

But he knew the different intonations of her yeahs. "I'm sorry," he told her.

"What should you be sorry for? I'm the one who cheated on you." He could hear the tears in her voice. He wanted nothing more than to swim through the telephone and be on the other side of the continent.

"I should have been more of a stand up guy. You wanted to keep the baby and I wasn't ready. I---"

"Stop this, Matt. Stop talking. I can't take this right now." Her voice. He put his finger on it when he heard that tone before.

"You're pregnant?" She stayed silent. She was quiet long enough that he knew he was correct. "I know it's not mine. I don't know what you're planning or what that guy is planning, but I'll help you out. I'll do whatever I can. I'll move back there and I'll help you raise him. I know I won't be his dad, or her dad but I'll---"

"I already had the procedure. This morning I had another fucking abortion."

So that was what he heard in her voice. "I'm sorry."

"Why the fuck should you be sorry?"

"I know it was difficult the first time and I know I don't like to hear you sad. So, I'm sorry that you had to go through that again."

"That was sweet of you to say. But it was my decision."

"I know, but I could have put in more of an effort to tell you that we should have kept it."

"Matt, I don't want to hear this right now."

"You're right, I'm sorry."

"Stop apologizing."

"Ok, sorry for all the sorries. How do you feel?"

"I feel so stupid and guilty, but my body feels fine. They gave me painkillers."

There was no sensitive way for Matt to correct the meaning of his question, so he was blunt. "I'm glad you feel okay, but that wasn't what I meant. I put the phone on my bed, how does my bed feel?"

"It feels strange and comforting at the same time."

"Like us."

"Yeah, I guess like us."

October 23, 1999
A New Sheriff in Town

Matt was at the information kiosk when Katie told him something. "Hey, Matt there's a guy in the art section doing weird stuff."

Matt's first thought was that Jay had stopped by and had taken his shoes off to read. "What kind of weird stuff?"

"It smells like he's smoking or something."

"You want to watch the info booth and I'll take a look?" He walked down the aisle. He hated being a nag. He was always annoyed how many times he had to remind people when they were closing. Excuse me sir, Borders will be closing in thirty minutes. Excuse me ma'am, Borders will be closing in ten minutes. Sir, we're closing now, you're going to have to leave.

The customer in question was a young guy. Matt's age give or take a year with a backpack strapped on. He had a huge coffee table Picasso book splayed out on the ground with a pile of CD's next to him. "Hi, can I help you find something?"

The guy panicked for a moment. "Oh no, I've found everything I need. Thanks."

Matt surveyed the situation and went into his memory banks to figure out exactly what was going on here. "Okay, let me know if you need anything." He rushed back to his station and grabbed the phone to call up to the manager's desk. It was Dan who picked up. Matt tried to speak in a hushed tone even though he was incredibly excited. "Hey, it's Matt. You know, how we keep finding those jewel cases in the art section? The guy responsible is here, burning the CD's out of them now."

"I'll be right down," Dan said.

It seemed like it was already too late though. The perp was walking toward the front of the store. Matt gave him a nod and the guy quickly looked away. Just to check his hunch Matt walked back to the art section and sure enough there was that pile of CD's hidden exactly where they found the burnt out plastic cases before. Matt appreciated the thief's musical taste, but he wasn't going to let him get away with this.

Dan had made his way down to the first floor. Matt led him into the café section where their guy was looking at the pastry selections in the café. "That's him," Matt said almost jumping up and down. "Do you want me to search his bag or should you?"

"We can't do that."

"Can't do what?"

"Search his bag. It's corporate policy."

"I'm sure everything he did is all on video."

"We've got to wait until the sensors go off when he leaves."

"He rips the CD's out of what makes the sensors go off. There's not going to be any alarm."

"It's a potential lawsuit. It's not worth it to corporate for thirty dollars of merchandise."

The guy headed for the exit. Matt took a big breath, but to no avail. The guy walked out silently except for Matt's verbal alarm. "He's getting away!"

"Why do you care? I've never seen you so excited. This is the only time I've ever seen you have a pulse about anything work related."

That was a good question. Why was he so into catching the guy? Matt always fancied himself as anti-authoritarian, but he never wanted so badly anything in his life as to confront this guy. Not to bust him necessarily, but just to let him know, "I'm on to you. You think you're the smartest guy in the room? Not on my watch." But this job couldn't even afford him that pleasure.

A gloom descended upon him on the pointlessness of his day to day life. He answered phone calls of customers seeking books knowing they could train a monkey to do what he was doing. Matt realized that was an insult to monkeys, because a monkey was alive and all life had meaning. Much worse they could program a robot to replace Matt. An automated voice could tell you where to find things and probably even make recommendations. Surely it could work the cash register and send off an alarm to tell the other robots when to take their ten minute breaks.

There was one ray of sunshine as Saturday night drew nearer. It was his nightly phone calls with Erin. He didn't want to think what his phone bill would be. Even with the deal he found where he could call for five cents a minute, they had been stretching the boundaries of how long two people could stay on the phone together.

So as Matt clocked out and drove the few minutes to his apartment his mood lightened. It hit its peak when he heard Erin's voice. "Hey," was all she had to say, and all felt right in the world.

"What's up!!!!" he hissed like they did in that beer commercial.

"How are you doing?"

"Good, now that I'm talking to you. I wish though instead of my voice just being transmitted through the phone that I could step into it and come out on your side." He always said that with every single one of their phone calls.

"That would be cool," she said.

Matt couldn't help but notice there wasn't that flow that had been present the past week when they'd been talking every spare moment they had. Maybe she was feeling down due to what she went through. She had no class or work and he knew as well as anyone how idle hands let the devil into your thoughts. "You feel okay?"

"Yeah."

"Did you do anything today?"

"Just worked on my Ancient Civilizations midterm."

"Time travel is always fun. So, you're doing that all night?"

"I might go to the movies. Maybe I'll finally see *Fight Club*."

"Nice. You'll love it. I saw it again without the psychedelics and it held up completely. It's fucking genius. It puts everything that's wrong with the world in cinematic form. You're going by yourself? Some of your friends, I don't know if they'll like all the---"

"I'm going with Chad."

"Who's Chad?" It took Matt a moment, a silent moment to realize who Chad was. Then it hit him like the weight of the world. "I thought you weren't talking with him."

"We spoke. We have spoken."

"But he wasn't there for you. You said you had to go by yourself to have the abortion. You said he couldn't even be man enough to be by your side for that."

"Things are more complicated. People are more complicated. You know that."

"No, I don't know anything. Obviously, I don't know anything. Okay, I don't want to hold you up, I'm sure you need to ready yourself for the hot date."

"Don't be an asshole, Matt."

"I can't help it. Just remember this time to use a condom." He hung up the telephone and looked around the apartment to see which wall he should bang his head into until he could feel nothing. He chose the one that the couch leaned against as he heard the phone ring leading to Erin leaving a profanity laced message.

October 26, 1999
Best Laid Plans

"Where have you been?" Jay asked Matt from behind the information desk.

"Here since the morning."

"No, I mean the last couple days. I thought you had Sunday's and Monday's off. I tried calling you a thousand times."

A customer stood behind Jay fidgeting impatiently. Matt asked Jay, "Can you go outside? I have a break in few minutes."

"Yeah, sure."

A few minutes later Matt told Jay the whole sorry confluence of events involving Erin. Jay simply couldn't understand. "Man, there's beautiful women everywhere. Look, hot chick walking across the street. Look, another hot chick driving that Honda."

"I thought it was if you want to be happy for the rest of your life get yourself an ugly wife."

"There's ugly women all around us too. What I mean is it seems apparent it's not meant to work between you two. Either she likes messing with your emotions or the universe likes messing with your emotions, but either way you need to figure out a way to move on or life is going to continue to be a struggle."

"Not everyone is gifted with your ability to love and leave."

"Sure, they are. They just need to find the right mix of drugs."

"It's not just that. It's like what the hell am I doing here? I'm working every day and what's the point? Just to squeak by? They don't even care about my talents. The other day I caught someone stealing CD's and they wouldn't even let me bust him. They let him walk right through the door and said it would be too much of a bother to pursue."

"Why don't you come down to Jamaica with me?"

"You're going again?"

"Yeah, that's why I was trying to get a hold of you. I wanted to see if I could leave some stuff at your place."

"When are you leaving?"

"Whenever Rasta Rick is ready. Probably the next week or two."

"I'd have to let work know."

"Fuck them. You said they don't appreciate you."

"You're right. I shouldn't even give notice. I should be a mystery of where I went. The problem is they wouldn't even care. I'm just another cog in the service economy. Rasta Rick is cool with me going?"

"Yeah, he was saying an extra pair of hands would be a big help. Plus, Rasta likes you. He told me a bunch of times how he thought you had a wise aura."

"That's nice of him. But I don't know how to sail."

"It's easy, there's a motor and a computerized navigation system. You'll learn on the way."

"I thought he was all worried about Y2K destroying all the computers."

"That's why he's trying to make as many runs as he can before the end day. Plus, he's got maps and the boat has sails."

Matt made a big decision. "Fuck it. Let's do it."

"My man." Jay gave Matt a big hug.

"I'm going to tell Dan I'm quitting right now."

"Hold on, why don't we stick it to them where they don't care that it hurts?"

Matt went back to work after Jay told him his plan. A couple hours later when Matt was working the register it all came to fruition. Matt saw Jay in line with a stack of CD's almost going to the roof. He took a deep breath and tried to time it perfectly so he would be the one to check Jay out. "Good afternoon, did you find everything you needed during your Borders experience?"

"Yeah, thanks."

Matt went through the pile of CD's. He only scanned every third one though he went through the motions of charging for every single one, making sure to unlock all the security cases. Godfrey who was working the register next to Matt complimented the band on Jay's shirt. "Public Enemy? That's a cool shirt."

"Thanks."

Matt didn't like someone paying attention to this transaction even if the worker smoked a blunt on every one of his breaks. "That will be sixty-three eighty seven.'

Jay paid him with nearly exact change. "I'm three cents short."

"You don't have a bill that I can give you change for?"

"Oh, yeah."

Matt wanted to kill Jay. He let him have it when he met him after work. "What were you thinking? I thought we were going to do that with only like four or five CD's."

"Yeah, I got a little crazy. Sorry. You should have charged me more for them. That was like three hundred dollars worth of music you gave me for free."

"Not free. I charged you something."

"No. I went back and returned the CD's you had me pay for."

Matt took a big sigh as he saw his car in the distance. Jay told him to open up the hatchback. Matt was about to ask why when Jay began loading two bikes that were locked to a stop sign near the car. "Where did you get those?" Matt asked.

"This is what Rasta Rick ships to Jamaica. He let me buy a couple of them for a good price. I figured you might want one too. Don't worry. I covered yours, they were only like fifty bucks each."

That seemed fair enough to Matt, not that he figured he would have much need for a bicycle while sailing on the seven seas.

October 31, 1999
The Spooky Unknown

It was Halloween, so it seemed if ever there was a day where the supernatural could occur this was it. Matt and Jay took the two bikes on a ride toward Key Biscayne. The big bridge was tough to climb, but the rush on the way down made the work well worth it. Jay pointed out the old drawbridge that once made the trip to Key Biscayne much more of a mission. You could wait forever if a line of boats wanted to get through.

As they biked into Bill Baggs Park looking for bodies of water that might contain the ingredients of the Fountain of Youth they spoke about what they should dress up as for Halloween. Matt thought with his hat he could pull off a decent Indiana Jones impersonation. Jay suggested maybe they could be zombies or vampires. Finally, they decided with their upcoming smuggling trip, they should be pirates. The hangers in Matt's closet could easily function as hooks. The question was where to get eyepatches?

Matt asked Jay for details about his last trek going in and out of Jamaica. "The hardest part," Jay said, "was the monotony. You're out there with nothing to do, nowhere to go except for your destination. But I figure it's good preparation for when the computers all crash and distractions won't always be so easily available."

"Did you see Jamaica at all?"

"No, it was kind of all business. I didn't even set foot on the island. We anchor the boat, row out with the goods and head back."

A little danger was just what Matt needed to push him out of his comfort zone and remind him that he was alive. "I told this guy at work what we were doing---"

"What? You can't! Anyone could try to jack us or narc on us."

"No, I mean this." Matt said pointing at the water he was drinking before spitting it out. "This guy Steve said there's salt water crocodiles back here."

"Bullshit. This is where I grew up. I never heard about a Key Biscayne crocodile."

Matt continued the story. "Yeah, he said the crocodile was laying out on the beach and they had to haul one of those bulldozers they use to clear the seaweed to pick him up to move him back into the water."

"Hell," Jay said, "I guess if we live in a world where there's a Fountain of Youth you have to be open to believing in sea monsters."

As they biked back Matt wanted to pass by a spot Steve had told him about. It took some sleuthing and some wrong turns to find the place on Virginia Key, but Jimbo's was just as his co-worker had described. A bunch of ramshackle buildings and trailers nestled on the bay right next to a sewage plant. Jay was surprised he did not know about it as they gave a guy five bucks for two bottles of beer.

They sat on a park bench overlooking the dock. They were within hearing distance of a couple sunburnt drunks arguing about the bocce ball game they were playing. Matt stretched out his tired feet as he tried to swat away a mosquito. "What if this is it?" he asked Jay.

"What if this is what?"

"This is all we get. We have... or at least I have all these expectations of what life is supposed to be. But what if this is as good as it gets? A beer in the shade with a friend?"

For a moment there was nothing but silence. Matt wondered what profound or mocking answer Jay would say. But then Jay silently walked toward the water. "Dude, is that a crocodile?"

Matt stood to see where Jay was pointing at. There was something large swimming under the surface, but from that distance he could not say whether it was something rare and dangerous or something common and friendly.

November 4, 1999
Make a Wish

Matt asked for the day off from work way in advance. It was his birthday. Twenty three years since he was brought on to this Earth. He always gave November 4th extra significance. Not that he was egocentric or anything, but it was nice to have a day all to himself. Whenever anyone asked him his favorite song what immediately came to mind was "Happy Birthday!" The idea of cake and candles and a free wish couldn't help, but to make him happy.

On this birthday he slept until eleven and when he awoke was surprised to see no messages had been left on his voice mail. Then he remembered there was a three hour difference between Florida and California. All his people were surely just waking up and would undoubtedly call him later.

Matt took a bike ride out to the bay. He looked out in the middle of the water and couldn't believe that in any day he would be in the middle of that sea on an adventure. He stopped at Pollo Tropical and ordered a breakfast of black beans, rice, and plantains. This would be his year he told himself. Twenty-three would bring great things. Assuming of course society would make it into the New Year.

Matt made it back home and was surprised to see no messages. He went outside with a paperback copy of *Jesus' Son* and tried to read about a lost drug addict, but it kept eating at him. Here it was almost two in the afternoon and not one person called to wish hearty congratulations on making it around the sun one more time.

For a second he figured he deserved it. He left them all behind, didn't he? He wanted to be his own man by moving across the country and now he was his own man.

But still, come on, not even his sister called? Not even his mom and dad who brought him into this reality. He went over to the telephone, unsure of who exactly he was going to chastise for not acknowledging his special day, but planning to tear into someone. But when he picked up the phone, there was no dial tone, no busy signal, no nothing. He looked at the unopened mail with writing on the envelope that said past due and went to knock on John's door.

"What?" he heard John yell.

Matt opened the door to see John had taped black garbage bags over the windows. "Did you forget to pay the phone bill?'

"What time is it?"

"Did you?"

"Maybe"

"What did you do with the money I gave you?" John rolled out of the mattress on the floor and counted out some loose bills that were in his pant's pocket.

Matt's shoulders fell to the floor. "It's my birthday."

"Happy birthday."

Matt felt it was too petty to yell at John that his birthday couldn't be so happy if he didn't have the tool allowing people to communicate with him that he should have a happy birthday. Instead he just said, "Let's go to the phone company and pay them to turn it back on."

"Okay," John said as he tied up his tennis shoes. "I'll drive. I get really good mileage."

Matt didn't argue with him. He hopped in the passenger seat of what looked like an ordinary sedan. "How many miles per gallon?"

"It depends." John said. "If I'm driving really efficiently on the highway and squeeze behind a truck to block all the headwind…maybe eighty miles a gallon."

"Bullshit."

"It's true. I once filled up and drove to West Palm and the gauge barely moved. It was like eighty miles and to be honest I don't even think I used a gallon."

Matt felt dumbstruck. He was about to explain how his car did the same thing, when the tank was full, it took a while for the arrow on his gauge to realize any gas was used, but he stopped himself. It would be like telling a newborn puppy there was no Santa Claus.

They went into the phone company's office and paid the past due bill which was over a hundred dollars. The lady at the desk said they would turn it back on first thing in the morning. "You can't do it now?" Matt begged.

"Too late." She shook her head.

"But it's my birthday."

"Felicidades," she said which to Matt's non-bilingual ears might as well have been a Santeria curse. Right when nothing could make him feel worse, John opened his mouth. "Oh, your friend stopped by this morning. The one who's always sleeping on the couch."

"When?"

"I don't know. This morning. You weren't here. He waited for a bit. He said he was in a rush."

"When I was out biking?"

"I don't know. Maybe?"

"Fuck!" Matt pointed John toward the docks. He went to the pay phone and left a number for Rasta Rick's pager to no avail. As he sat on the front of John's hood waiting to either get a call back or to see Rasta Rick row into their vicinity, Matt saw a sunburnt guy hosing off his feet and flip-flops. He'd noticed the guy before because he wore hats made out of palm tree fronds. Matt asked him, "Hey, do you know Rasta Rick?" The guy looked him up and down. "He docks his boat out there. He has a wife and---"

"Yeah man, Rasta Rick took off to Jamaica this morning. He'll be back in like a week or two. You need some weed?"

Matt's head hung lower than it had in quite some time. It had been almost a week since he felt this disappointed. John suggested they grab dinner at Monty's which overlooked the bay. They secured a table. John ordered a hamburger. Matt ordered the fries since that was all he could presently afford. "This is the worst birthday I ever had."

"Sorry,' John said. He took a couple bites into his sandwich before adding, "Mine was when I turned eight and my parents told me they were getting divorced."

November 9, 1999
Suspicious Minds

Growing up a California kid Matt thought he had been slightly deprived of seasons. He looked with envy as a kid watching the Christmas specials with snow in the landscape, but Florida was even less seasonal. Here it was eighty degrees and the drug store already had their Christmas decorations ready. Matt bought a package of candy canes to go with the toilet paper that was his incentive for leaving the house. Halfway home he felt a little silly that he tried to be environmentally conscious in saying no to a bag. Holding the toilet paper and candy cane box in his left hand made steering the bike more difficult than it would have been with two hands.

Matt made it home in time to eat lunch and then bike to work. Matt was willing to forgive Jay for leaving to Jamaica without him only because of the bicycle. It was freeing and gave him a way to pedal out his frustrations. Since he started commuting to work on it, a few rude comments had been made about Matt's body odor. But he felt an offensive aroma was a worthy fuck you, in exchange for a society whose economic system forced him to spend forty hours a week cooped inside a corporate chain store.

Matt was scheduling himself as much as possible to work in the back where he shelved and organized books. Lately he felt like not dealing with people.

Unfortunately, that jerk off Rob was on the phone. Rob was for a time a fellow lead manager who recently received a promotion. Now mad with power, Rob had chastised Matt for reading a book while working at the information desk.

It wasn't until a couple moments after Rob walked away from the scolding that Matt realized he should have said, "I work at a fucking book store. You should be encouraging me to read on the job!"

But he didn't say that. So, it annoyed him even more to hear Rob speak on the phone with what seemed to be his girlfriend on what they should eat for dinner. They talked about going out or ordering a pizza.

They were very close to making some spaghetti, but finally decided to have some cereal with milk for their final meal of the night.

As sad as a dinner of cereal sounded, Matt realized he had lately been eating similarly. He used to love cooking. He had a couple of cool cookbooks he'd found in thrift stores that he messed around with. One was recipes from a hippie commune with all kinds of groovy vintage photos of the food and the long haired people that cooked it. Sometimes he and Erin wouldn't eat all day knowing they were going to prepare a huge meal for dinner. Now it was hard for Matt to find the incentive to cook when it would be just him eating the meal. Then he remembered even if he did want to cook something from that book it was too late, he left all those cookbooks with her in California.

"Fucking bullshit." The door to the back room swung open violently. Matt looked back to see it was Swain, a young guy cursing and stomping around.

"What happened?" Matt asked him.

"Dan had me up in his room with Gary and Ken and all the other bosses. They're telling me all this bullshit that they know I'm stealing from the store."

"What did you tell them?"

"I told the motherfuckers to prove it. They didn't have shit. I asked them why they always accusing people with dark skin. I turned that shit around on them. They started acting all defensive. They said they heard I been stealing shit."

"Have you?"

"Fuck you. Have you?"

Matt decided not to answer the question just as Swain didn't answer either. There would be silence amongst thieves. "So that was it?"

"No, they sweat me in there. Telling me I wouldn't get in any trouble if I told them what I took and who else been taking shit."

"What did you tell them?"

"I told them fuck you."

"Really?"

"Fuck, yeah."

Matt didn't believe Swain, but it put a smile on his face imagining the managers' faces when being cursed out. "You know I caught some guy stealing a few weeks ago and they wouldn't let me catch his bag. They said it was opening them up for a lawsuit. Then they go around and accuse the people that build this company."

"Yeah, man, they going after a bunch of people. You know that fine Brazilian girl who just started? They brought her in right before me. Her eyes were all red like she was crying and shit. Those fuckers are on a mission to bust someone."

It took a few minutes, but Matt started to feel funny in his stomach. He'd been acting a little sloppy lately. He of course hooked Jay up with that huge discount, but he also lately started taking books and CD's with him just about every day when he left. He did it smooth, like he brought them in with him to work and was just taking them home where they rightfully belonged. But he knew there were video cameras all over the store. All it would take was a patient eye and they could undoubtedly rewind and catch him.

When it was his turn to work the register he couldn't help but pay attention to the managers' every move. A woman asked him if his name was really Tex as his nametag said. Most times he would have caught that she was flirting with him and respond with a long winded story about how his parents conceived him in a lonely motel room in the Lone Star State, but he was so preoccupied about his sins he just told her, "No, it's not."

During a spell when there were no customers Godfrey who was working the register next to him asked, "They take you up there yet to give you the inquisition?"

"They asked if you were stealing too?"

"Yep. I told them I don't do that," Godfrey said in his flat affect. "They asked me who does. I told them I keep my head straight ahead and I don't see nothing except for a margarita when I clock out."

That calmed Matt down a little. They didn't have anything on anyone. They were just hoping someone would break. He would keep it cool and like everyone else would be released without any punishment. But as he worked and counted how much money was coming into the store he started to be offended. In one hour he sold two thousand dollars worth of books and music. Out of that they only had to pay him seven fifty. He was worth only half of one percent of what he sold and for that they would be so petty as to give him a hard time for taking what really should be his. When he saw Dan, he couldn't help himself. "It's not right what you're doing."

"What are you talking about?" Dan asked with an annoyed air.

"Treating employees like thieves. It's not right. We work hard and don't earn much, the least you could do is show us a little respect."

"You don't know what you're saying. I didn't take you as someone who listens to gossip. Just don't worry. It has nothing to do with you."

Matt almost gave himself away by saying out loud, "It doesn't?" But he didn't say that, still he felt he might have put some suspicion on himself so he kept talking. "It does have something to do with me. You mistreat one of the workers, you mistreat us all."

"Ugh." Matt had never heard someone in real life make that sound which he had previously only read in newspaper comic strips. "Fine! Next time you think you catch someone stealing I'll let you stall them while we call the police. That what this is about?"

"Yes. Yes, it is. Thank you. That is all I wanted to hear," Matt said and then watched as Dan asked Godfrey to return upstairs for another round of questioning.

November 13, 1999
Maybe?

Matt had given up on the fairer sex. Erin of course had moved on. Marylise he kept trying to call, but she kept saying work was keeping her very busy. He figured there was something repulsive about him that no woman wanted around. It was to his great surprise then when a very thin woman with a unique fashion sense came to his register. Her eyelids were painted in two different colors, one green, one blue. Her hair was spiky and she had a smile that made Matt think of the singer Bjork, only if she was on heroin.

She was buying Albert Camus' *The Stranger*. "I just read this." Matt told her with pride.

"What did you think?" she asked.

"I didn't understand it all, but what I did I loved."

"It's about life and death. If you understood those things you wouldn't be working at a cash register collecting money."

"You're right. And I'm not supposed to be here."

"Where should you be?"

"I should be in the middle of the ocean right now on my way back from smuggling pounds and pounds of marijuana."

She laughed at that. "You are more interesting than you appear."

"Thank you," Matt responded. "You are exactly as interesting as you appear."

"Would you like to go have a drink with me?"

"I'm working," he reminded her. For the first time during their interaction he noticed the impatient customer in line behind her. "My lunch break is in a half hour if you don't mind waiting."

"Good," she said, "Just so you know though, I am married so we can't fuck or anything." It all happened so fast that he didn't have time to get nervous. But as she walked away anxiety crept over him. By being so blunt was she really being coy and she did want to fuck? He always had heard about these kinds of low key love affairs and even watched a couple adult videos that acted out such an interaction. Two strangers cross paths and moments later find themselves naked in an inconspicuous spot exchanging bodily fluids. Matt suddenly felt completely out of his element and looked around desperately for anyone to give him advice. But it was soon seven o'clock and for the closing shift that was time for lunch.

She was reading the free weekly paper, *Street Miami*. Matt tried to continue the appearance of being witty by asking, "You already finished the book you bought?"

"I've already read it. It's for my sister. She's in high school and they don't give her anything interesting to read. Erica."

It took Matt a second to realize she was introducing herself. It wasn't until she kissed him on the cheek and he could smell her perfume and cigarettes that he said his name. "Matthew." He was in a sophisticated situation, so he might as well give the sophisticated version of his name instead of the usual Matt.

They walked to The Hungry Sailor. He only had an hour, but he didn't tell her that. He figured this might be a tryst that would be worth getting fired over. She told him her backstory. She was from Argentina where she waited tables. She met her husband while there on vacation. "I thought he was an asshole at first. And he still is."

"But he's rich?" Matt guessed.

"Yes. Very rich. He wanted me to move here to Miami. I said only with my sister."

"So now you're happily married?"

She deflected the question and asked Matt about his past. He told her he moved out here from California and was unsure what he was doing. "I read a lot of books, I meet a lot of strangers, and I guess I spend a lot of time figuring out what to do with myself."

"You're a seeker," she said. "Good. What are you looking for?"

"Meaning I guess. And love and a good time."

"Those are three very different things. Have you ever read Alberto Moravia? No, of course not, you went to school in America. He's an Italian writer. My Grandfather met him once before he moved from Italy to Argentina. He has characters like you. Lost and at sea. He has one book called *Boredom* about such a seeker. He said boredom was a detachment from reality."

"I like that," Matt said as he finished his second beer. "I'll have to see if they have that book in the store. Oh man, what time is it?"

"Do you have to go back to work?"

"Yeah. I mean no, not if you want to do something."

"I have to pick up my sister from her friend's house. Then we are meeting my husband. Here…" she wrote down her phone number on a napkin and placed it in his hand. "Call me sometime and we can talk."

Matt nodded his head. He walked back to work a little tipsy, but excited with possibility. He clocked back in and sought out *Boredom*.

November 14, 1999
Maybe Not

"Boredom is detachment from reality," was indeed how the book began. Matt found himself devouring it. He spent every spare moment whether working or not burrowing through the novel of existential dread, of misbegotten love, of loneliness, of quiet desperation. He could relate to all of it and more. So when Matt found himself getting to those final two words of "The End," he rushed to the telephone to tell Erica by virtue of the book she had recommended that she knew him so well.

As one ring followed another Matt was all excitement and comfort but then a masculine voice answered on the other end.

"Hello."

"Hi, is Erica there."

"Who is this?"

"This is Matt. I met her at the bookstore the other day." Then he remembered, "Matthew."

"Excuse me?"

"Matthew. She knows me as Matthew, not Matt."

There was some muffled talk on the other line. Words were being shared, but Matt could not make out what they were as though someone's hand was covering the mouthpiece of the phone. Finally, he heard Erica's voice, "Hello?"

"Hi Erica, it's Matthew. From Borders bookstore?"

"I know who you are. What do you want?"

"I finished the book. *Boredom*. It was---"

"It's Sunday morning."

Matt looked at the clock. It was actually a couple minutes to one. "Sorry, I didn't mean to wake you. I just finished it and had the day off and thought maybe you could meet me for a coffee of a beer and talk about the book."

"I'm with my husband."

"You could bring him along if you want." Matt had no idea why he said that. He could not think of a situation he less wanted to be involved in then to awkwardly meet her guy.

"Thank you, but we are planning to lay around in bed all day."

"Okay. Maybe another time."

"Yes, another time. Good-bye."

Before she hung up the phone he could hear a raised voice. A moment after there was nothing to hear but a dial tone. He crumpled up the paper with her phone number written on it and threw it in the garbage can. This Sunday would be his and his alone.

He went back into his bedroom and collapsed on his bed. He now reflexively knew where exactly to plop down so he wouldn't feel the coils of the springs.

For a moment he tried to remember what it felt like to have someone lay next to him on a lazy Sunday afternoon, but then he stopped himself. Self-pity was a very easy hole to lose himself in. He stopped staring into space and instead paid attention of what his eyes were gazing into, the bare walls of his room. Some might find it silly that months into his stay here he had done not a single thing to adorn them. The hat he bought in New Mexico hung on the rack on the back of his door, but other than that the room was white and plain. Part of it was out of laziness, another part was the idea that Matt had that his stay in these quarters were extremely temporary. That something better would come along any moment.

But the main reason Matt realized right then why he had done nothing to decorate what confined him was that he would then have admitted that there are walls that boxed him in. By refusing to acknowledge their existence, he could rebel and pretend that his surroundings were unformed. The future was limitless. There was nothing holding him in and no one holding him back from doing whatever it was he wanted or needed, except for a lack of imagination. That gave him comfort. Even if he had to admit paint or a taped on poster could make his room a little cheerier.

November 21, 1999
Pie Makes Everything Bitter

Jay persuaded Matt to take the drive down Grand Avenue to the weekly farmer's market for his lunch break. Matt did not appreciate it because it was always a pain to find parking on a Saturday. But Jay promised he would make it worth his time. Matt figured that meant Jay would have the dignity to buy lunch for his part in Matt missing out on the Jamaican adventure.

As he made a left toward the tent Jay waved him down. "Back up right into there."

Matt did as he was directed and pulled up next to a truck. Before Matt could jump out of his car Jay had already opened the hatchback and he and a bearded man began loading produce into the car.

There were boxes of avocados and mangos, dried apricots, cashews, and fresh mamey. A fruit pie followed by a vegetable pie were thrown into the mix as well.

"Do you like papayas, bro?" the bearded guy asked Matt before he could be sure of what was going on.

"Yeah, sure."

"Here you go, on the house." The stranger threw the thin melon sized fruit before Matt was ready to catch it. It fell on the ground harmlessly. "Is that good, Jay?"

"Yeah," Jay said, jumping in the car with Matt. Before Matt had a chance to ask why he had a car filled with fruit Jay began explaining Rasta Rick had to pay him for his services in weed. Jay had more weed then he could smoke, cook, sell or even store. He had to get creative with disposing it and thus traded a large amount for a credit with the local farmer's market

As he drove back Matt shook his head. His parking spot had been taken. He made a right to circle the block when Jay panicked. "Where are you going?"

"Looking for a spot. I have to go back to work."

"We need to get to your house first. All this stuff will go bad if you leave it in the car." Matt took a deep sigh and put his foot on the gas. Matt tried as fast as he could to load everything from his car into his refrigerator, but the three flights of stairs and the heavy crates made it a slower enterprise then he would have liked. Especially when Jay kept wanting to tell Matt about the trip.

"I get it. You had an awesome time."

"It kind of sucked man. Rasta Rick is a little nuts."

"I need to get back to work." Matt held Jay off from explaining what was seemingly obvious.

As Matt ran a deep yellow light even though it was already two minutes past when he should have clocked in Jay described Rasta Rick's eccentricities. "He talks to himself. I don't know if it's from smoking so much pot or all the sun. I thought he was praying at first or something, but he has debates and he takes both sides of the issue."

Matt thought he found a spot but his car clearly could not fit into it. Jay kept on, "Mostly he's talking about Y2K. I know he might be crazy, but it seems if there's even a one percent chance of it happening, it's better to prepare and... oh shit man we forgot one of the pies." Matt didn't even acknowledge that sentence. Jay pointed at it in the back and emphasized again, "It's going to go bad. We got to go back to your pad."

"I don't have time."

"Those things sell for forty bucks and it won't stay good without refrigeration for more than like a half hour."

"I don't fucking give a fuck about your pie."

Jay was speechless for once. He'd rarely seen Matt lose his cool. As Matt drove around the block again Jay tried to make amends. "I mean if you want to give me your keys I can drop you off and then go to your apartment to put the pie in the refrigerator."

"It's not about the fucking pie."

"I'm sorry. I wanted to wait for you. But Rasta Rick is a weird cat. He said Jahweh wanted us to leave right then and how can you argue with that. I tried to stall, but--"

"You're a fucking user. You're only around when you have a need for me. It's a little annoying and inconvenient." Matt stopped with that point. He was suddenly embarrassed for his outburst.

"That's the human condition, right? We're selfish creatures, all of us. I'm sorry for being like everyone else."

"Whatever." Matt saw someone pulling out and quickly took the spot. He grabbed the pie as he returned to his place of employment.

"What are you doing with that?"

Matt was of half a mind not to answer. He wanted to keep walking and let the whereabouts of his pie torture Jay for the next six hours, but Matt spoke. "They have a refrigerator in the break room."

It took all Matt had within him not to slam the pie on the ground when he heard Jay yell, "Don't forget about it when you leave."

November 25, 1999
Grace

As Matt spoke to his mom on the telephone and she wished him a happy Thanksgiving a certain amount of homesickness set in. He thought about late November Thursdays from his past and being rounded up by a couple other kids in the neighborhood. They would throw the football around and maybe get a three on three game that would only be stopped by the occasional passing car driving on their residential road.

"How much longer are you going to be out there?" Mom asked.

He didn't have an answer. None of this was planned and at the moment he wished he had not gone to the bar that particular night in August and cried his troubles to Jay. If he had chosen another spot or perhaps seen a movie that fateful night he would be at home preparing for a feast of turkey, sweet potatoes, stuffing, pumpkin pie, and not one, but multiple cranberry sauces.

When he told his mom he did not know how much longer his journey would last she said, "Well just remember we still haven't rented out your bedroom yet." When he thanked her facetiously she started describing how much rentals for rooms were currently going for in their neighborhood. "Where are you going to have Thanksgiving dinner?"

He told her he hadn't decided. That was kind of true though the only invitation he received was from Jay. But Matt was not sure how welcoming Uncle Jim would be.

His mom told him, "Whoever is lucky to have you over I am very jealous of." He was sure someone had said nicer words to him over the years, but at that moment it felt like the kindest words ever uttered in human history.

Matt lost himself in his box of the past, it was one of the few things he had taken with him. It was a cardboard container of little mementos he had picked up over the past few years. Much of it was made up of love letters he had received from Erin while she was studying abroad. Most noteworthy for him was a little comic strip he had drawn. Matt was a terrible artist, but the idea was clever enough, his crude penmanship did not affect it. It was titled "The Life of a Fruitfly." The first panel showed a clock reading 6:00 and a fruitfly being born. The second panel showed it reading 9:00 and the fruitfly eating a strawberry. 10:00 had the fruitfly going up to a female fruitfly and saying "hey baby." At noon he was eating again. At 3:00 the fruitfly is flying around with a thought balloon that read, "I have wasted my life." At 5:00 he eats some more. At 6:00 he lies dead. The final panel reads, "meanwhile" with the clock still reading 6:00 as another fruitfly is hatching.

It was late in the afternoon when Matt heard John open his door and lurk out to the hallway. "Happy Thanksgiving," Matt told him.

"It's Thanksgiving?" John asked. Matt nodded his head acknowledging there was always another step toward disconnect that he could take. "Happy Thanksgiving to you."

"What are you doing?"

"I don't know. Might go to work and perhaps compete."

All of a sudden, Matt felt bad for both himself and for John. "Do you want to maybe go to Jay's uncle's house for a Thanksgiving dinner?"

"I could do that."

Matt called Uncle Jim's house but received no answer. He decided not to leave a message and to just take the drive up to Fort Lauderdale. "We should bring something, shouldn't we?"

"I guess that is what people do," John agreed.

It was too late though for any of the supermarkets, they had all closed for the holiday. Eventually they saw a liquor store still open for business. They went halves on a bottle of rum that Matt remembered Uncle Jim pouring from.

Matt parked on the grass among the many cars he did not recognize and knocked on the door. Uncle Jim opened up. Matt said, "Happy Thanksgiving." And lifted up the bottle to show his good will.

Uncle Jim turned around and yelled, "Jose!" He blurted out more words in Spanish that didn't sound complimentary.

Jay came out and hugged Matt and John. "The boys made it. Happy Thanksgiving fellas. The last one we'll have lit up at night."

"What do you mean by that?" John asked.

There was an explanation of the end of civilization as we knew it coming in a little more than a month until Uncle Jim told them to shut up. Uncle Jim was focused on his Dolphins losing to the Cowboys.

The three guys went outside and met some more of Jay's extended family as they were cooking a turkey and setting up the outdoor table. "Get used to eating outside guys."

"Why?" John asked again.

"When the computers stop working on December 31, it's going to turn us back to the Stone Age. We won't have all the technology we're so dependent on."

"Well then wouldn't we want to eat inside," John proposed, "so that we were out of plain sight from other people that might try to attack us for our food?"

Jay was about to admit that was a good point when they were called to the table for dinner. There were twelve place settings of plastic ware and plates. The food, including several of the pies from the farmer's market, were all set up buffet style on a table, but before they dug in everyone held hands. A Spanish version of Grace was said or so Matt assumed. He did not ask what was being recited, nor was it translated, but he could only assume when he followed suit by putting his palms against Jay and John's hands that was what was going on. He closed his eyes and prayed for us all.

November 29, 1999
Aloha

It only took the after Thanksgiving weekend sale for Matt to finally get pretty good at wrapping gifts. He doubted he could manage wrapping a stuffed animal, a shirt, or any other irregularly shaped object, but he felt comfortable as far as rectangles or squares went. Whether it was a book, a CD, or the DVD's they started carrying he figured out how to do it. He could now eyeball the correct size that he should cut off from the roll and even if his estimation was slightly off, he knew now to origami the remainder into a pointed arrow that he could tape down, to adorn a completely aerodynamically wrapped gift.

Matt meant every jolly "Merry Christmas" he spouted out to a customer when he handed them their wrapped present even though the holiday was still close to a month away and it was eighty degrees.

Marylise had reached out to him the night before. He had written her off after calling several times with no response. But last night when he was desperate for some good news she called.

She had returned from Hawaii on her vacation and the guidebook he had recommended all those months ago was very helpful. She asked when they could get together. He suggested right that moment. She said how about tomorrow night.

Matt said perfect. Off at seven, he drove into Coral Gables toward the studio apartment she rented. Matt followed the directions that he had written on a scrap of paper. He parked on the road named after a Spanish city on the one lawn that didn't have those white concrete half domes that protected yards from cars doing what he just did. Jay told him those white half domes were called elephant turds. That sounded like a terrible name, but since he heard that he avoided touching them with either his feet or the wheels of his car, no matter how unsquishy their consistency was.

Matt walked to the back guest house and knocked three times. He heard her footsteps and was already as happy as he had been in a long time. Then she opened the door, stood on her tippie toes and put a flowered lei over his neck. She kissed each of his cheeks and Matt wouldn't have complained if he died right then.

"*Aloha*," she said in her French accent.

Matt was in shock. "This is for me?"

"Of course," she said. "I thought it would fit your shirt with flowers on it. Do you like it?"

"Of course." He had noticed lately he had picked up a bad habit of repeating phrases he had just heard. "I'm never going to take it off. Maybe to shower or to swim, but that's about it. So how was Hawaii?" She was about to answer but then he remembered something. "You're starving right? You said you don't like to eat dinner past seven and it's already almost eight."

"You have a great memory."

"I do. It's my blessing and my curse.'

"How so?" she asked as she walked with him to his car.

"I'm not really sure how it's a blessing, but it curses me because I'm always comparing everything now with something in the past."

"That could be bad," she agreed. She pointed toward a sushi restaurant on Miracle Mile. Matt gulped like he did at the restaurant from his first date, but he remembered he had been working a lot and had been stingy lately. He could afford a slight amount of decadence. She deserved it. She brought this flowered necklace all the way from four or five time zones away.

Marylise looked at him funny when he put the money in the meter and walked with her toward the restaurant with the lei still on him, but he was touched by her thoughtfulness.

They sat down and ordered edamame and a roll each and a hot bottle of sake. It was a Monday night so the restaurant was empty and there were not even many people walking on the sidewalk. She told him about Maui and laying on the beach and climbing a volcano. She also spent a couple days in Oahu. She didn't like how dirty and touristy Waikiki was, but she visited Pearl Harbor and thought that was a deep and solemn experience.

"It's cool that we've both been to the same place." She agreed even though she had a confused look on her face. "I mean I know we're at the same place now, but it's just cool we've also both been to Hawaii, you know?"

"It is." She started telling him about a hike to a waterfall where she had to walk through all this bamboo.

"That sounds magical," he said, feeling like he was in a fairy tale. But he suddenly didn't want the book to slam in his face again. "Did you end up going by yourself?"

"Yes."

"You didn't meet anyone there?'

"No. I talked to a couple people, but mostly I was by myself. It was good to give myself some time to think."

"Thinking is good.'

She told him about snorkeling and how she took surfing lessons.

"Did you get up on the board?"

"Yes."

"Awesome. One day you can come with me to Santa Cruz. It's perfect for beginners. The water's cold though so we'll have to find a wetsuit, but you'll love it."

She agreed to embark on that trip. He was ready to leave to California right that moment. Just like how he came out here, he would return home at a moment's notice. This time with the girl of his dreams by his side and a lei around his neck.

After indulging on green tea ice cream, Matt handed the waiter his bank card. He didn't look at the bill. He asked the waiter to include the tip and this way he would not put a price on the night that would be the opening chapter for the rest of his happy life.

Matt drove her home and as he parked in her front lawn he figured this time he would not move slow nor fast. He would not ask her if he could kiss her, nor would he kiss her without permission. If it was meant to be and it surely was, she'd come to him.

"It was really nice to see you," Matt said.

"Yes, it had been too long. I shouldn't go so long without seeing you. I will have to see if you are still wearing the lei."

"You could check up on me tomorrow."

"No, my boyfriend will be mad. I still haven't seen him since I came back yesterday."

"Boyfriend?"

"Yes," she began telling him some details but he wasn't really registering. He was a banker or something and he's even busier than her. Matt was driving before it really sunk in. She had kissed him on the cheek good night and he didn't say a word. He walked up to his apartment in complete and utter defeat. He took off his shirt to go to bed when he realized he was still wearing the lei.

He crumpled it up and threw it in the corner of his room

December 3, 1999
Youth

With nothing to do and the air finally losing the nastiest edge of its humidity, Matt went out for the grand bike ride. He pedaled under the canopies of Bayshore Drive. He made a right at the giant statue featuring a shark that advertised the Seaquarium. He kept going beyond the toll booth over one bridge past the windsurfers taking advantage of the breeze on Hobie Beach. He then took the climb above the monster bridge. The first time he attempted it, he had to get off and walk his way up. This time he took the bike down to its lowest gear and rode it up to the crest. He looked out both ways. To the north was the cityscape and the highrises of Downtown Miami, to the south was nothing but water, with the occasional lonely boat dotting his view.

Matt made it to the peak and then stopped doing any work. He let gravity take him down. There were no joggers or rollerbladers to avoid. He wondered how fast he was going. The cars were still passing him to his left, but he felt supersonic like he was in a different plane of existence. He kept going. He went through Virginia Key past the Seaquarium where a couple sign wielding protestors were trying to bring attention to the plight of the marine wildlife trapped in captivity. Matt agreed with their disdain, it was cruel and unusual for a creature to be jailed simply for a spectator's amusement. But he also felt a certain amount of envy for the orcas and dolphins with their lives decided for them constrained from wandering off on their own and getting lost.

He took the final bridge onto Key Biscayne and realized he would have to soon make a choice of where to head. The island was an endpoint. He could turn around and head back if he felt the need to keep moving, but there were no further bridges so that he could take himself further away. Matt decided to veer right into Calusa Park.

Matt remembered Jay's disappointment in how the present did not live up to his memories. What was once there no longer existed. To Matt the park was how it always appeared. He walked his bike on to the patch of grass where Jay remembered a little playhouse once was. Matt stood over it and tried to detect the energies of past performances, but felt nothing. He wheeled his bike into the mangroves and tried to find an area where they had not yet searched for the Fountain of Youth.

He came across a barbed wire fence and an electric generator. He was disappointed that this was all that he could feel, the static energy in the air and the nearly inaudible buzz of the creation and transference of power. Matt kept walking. He looked at the ground for little bodies of water they had not tried and felt like a fool.

This youth he was chasing, that he searched out of boredom with a sense of irony, was not even his youth, it was someone else's. What would this elixir even do? Would it prevent him from ever aging? Would drinking it turn him into a baby, or a younger version of himself? Would it take him back in time to the date of his birth in 1976? Maybe it would transport him to the time when he was happiest or maybe to the time of his life when he was most representative of youth?

He put down the bike when he reached water. His first instinct was to hop on the roots of the mangroves that extended outside the water to keep his shoes dry. As mosquitoes hovered in the air around him, he had a different idea. Without thinking he shovelled the muck with the palm of his hands into his mouth. This was quite different from how their previous searches for the Fountain of Youth went. Normally, they would take a sip, swish it around their mouth and then either spit it out or take the tiniest of swallows. But now he was chugging it. No more half measures. Either he had faith that these waters could save him, or he was an idiot and they would poison him.

As he kept drinking Matt almost became impressed at his will power. He was not allowing himself to taste the saltiness, nor the fragments of ooze that were present in every sip. This was what explorers circumnavigated half way across the world to consume. This was why he was here. He was not just a guy who worked for some corporate bookstore. He was not someone who only consumed, and never gave anything back to the world. He was not merely a cog in the machine. He was not just a speck of dust in the vast, uncaring universe. He was now doing something, not necessarily important, but something different, unique maybe not in the annals of human history, but something surely no one in modern times had tried. He would reap the rewards or suffer the punishment.

Eventually his gag reflex did not let him play the hero any more. He began to vomit all that he had just drank and more than that. His breakfast and some of yesterday's pre-bedtime snack came out of his mouth. As he coughed out everything, he heard footsteps. Normally, he would brace himself for a conflict. No one ever walked out in this swamp. It could be a crocodile or an angry vagrant, but Matt was too vulnerable at the time expelling the remnants of his stomach lining to even care. As he kept coughing he was too weak to even calculate the odds that the face that greeted him was a familiar one.

"Jesus, Matt, what the fuck?"

Jay helped Matt off his knees and moved him to a sitting position. When Matt finally could speak he asked, "Why are you here?"

"I'm doing what I'm always doing. Searching. What the hell are you doing here?"

"I guess the same thing." Matt didn't even care about the dribbles of vomit he could feel around his mouth. "I'm glad you came."

"Me too. What happened?"

"I drank from the water. I drank as much as I could take."

"What? I need to get an ambulance."

"No, we can see what it does, I think that was it. I think that was the Fountain of Youth."

Jay thought upon this. "I guess we do come into this world out of the womb a shitting, sloppy mess."

"What do you think it is going to do to me?"

"I hope nothing. I hope you're okay."

"If it is the Fountain of Youth what do you think it will do?'

"It's going to take you to the time when you were the youngest at heart. The time when you were the purest and the most innocent. The moment in your life when you were filled with the most potential to take in the wonders of being alive."

"Couldn't that be right now?"

"I don't see why not."

Matt began swatting at his arms, it felt like something was biting him. Matt's eyes slowly opened and he realized he was laying face first in the mud. He slowly stood himself up and began to feel the enormous pain of the tiniest of red ants crawling all over his arms. He used his hands to wipe the bugs as far off from him as he could. When he realized that was making the bugs climb on to his hands, he used his once white and now stained brown t-shirt to brush them all off.

"Jay," Matt called out. There was no answer.

Matt looked at the ground to see if he could decipher a second pair of shoeprints in the dirt, but his ants in the pants dance had done a number on making sense of the ground. He picked up his bicycle and wheeled it out of the swamp. There was still sunlight, but he could not figure out for how long he had lost himself.

He was grateful no one could see him. He must have looked like a horror show with the mud and the vomit and the whitehead pimples that were already forming from the ant bites. When he got to asphalt he sat on the bike and pedaled. Even though his body was light on crucial fluids necessary for survival, the ride back was easy. He was fueled by all that he had to think about.

December 10, 1999
Beats Working

"Tell her," Jay told Matt.

"He did. It's all true," Matt verified.

"I don't care if you sailed to the moon, it's not my boat to give you," Mayra told him for the umpteenth time.

Jay eyed the vessel as though it was already his. They were blasting the new Beastie Boys box set that Matt was finally able to walk out of the store with. Mayra was trying to host as many people as many nights as she could. It seemed the house had sold and she would have to be out by the middle of January.

"Don't move out until the last minute." Jay had warned her. Mayra asked why. This led to Jay explaining how civilization was about to fall which finally resulted in his asking the question he had wanted to ask since he first set eyes on the boat with the words "Beats Working" painted on its bow.

"You're invited to come with me. Water is the safest place to be. You don't want to be around when nothing is working and everyone is panicking and fighting over what limited rations we have."

"But if like you're saying, planes will be falling out of the sky because they're going to stop working, couldn't one hit you in the middle of the water?"

"If you think like that," Jay told her, "you'll never get out of bed. An asteroid could hit the Earth tomorrow morning, a nuclear bomb could malfunction, a super virus could escape from one of the labs scientists are experimenting in, any of this could happen any moment."

"Oh, you're one of those?"

"One of those people who prepares?"

"No, one of those paranoid fucking burnouts."

"Is that what I am?" he asked and his tone started getting flirtatious and Matt was not surprised at all to see that Jay was now shamelessly kissing her.

He walked over to the keg they all chipped in on and refilled his red plastic cup. What was the saying, whether by hook or by crook? He knew Jay well enough that if he wanted something, he got it even if he had to fuck his way to his goal.

As he pumped the keg he thought he saw a ghost, or maybe a zombie. But then he realized it was Steve who with his raspy voice said, "What's up Matt?"

"Hey man, I don't think I've ever seen you outside of the store."

"There's no hockey game tonight I figured what the hell, might as well socialize with the future generation." He took a drag from his cigarette and then pointed out the most conspicuous aspect of the low key gathering. "Looks like your pal and Mayra are getting along."

Matt turned to see that Mayra was sitting on Jay's lap on the pool chair dry humping and getting each other's saliva all over the place. Steve turned the focus back to small talk. "You going back to California for the holidays?"

"No, I don't think so. I'm kind of low on cash."

"Why don't you hit up your parents?'

"My mom offered, but I feel like since I dragged myself out here if I want to get back I should figure out my own way."

"That's admirable. Stupid, but admirable. Take advantage of people's generosity while you can."

"I guess that's good advice."

"There's something different about you," Steve said.

"You're the first person that's noticed."

"What is it? Did you cut your hair or did you fuck?"

"Neither," Matt said as he drowned his throat with beer and started pumping up the keg to refill his cup. "I drank from the Fountain of Youth."

Matt thought he was being bold, playful, and maybe a little outrageous by saying what he just did. He couldn't imagine what kind of response Steve would give him. Last on his list for guesses would be world weariness. "I remember when I used to do that."

December 16, 1999
The Past and the Future

"I love you," Matt said to himself in the mirror. It was a new habit he figured was healthy to pick up. He always felt better when he heard those three words. If there was no one in arm's length that could say that to him, he might as well say it to himself.

He took the bicycle to work. His gas tank was low, plus the exercise put him in a better mood anyway. Sometimes coming back on the bike after a day in the coal mines didn't seem so appealing, but better to be sorry than safe.

Matt clocked in and took his turn at the register. It wasn't until his turn at the information booth that something of note happened.

She walked up in a tank top and shorts, it took a moment before they recognized each other. He looked into her eyes and after a second he realized they shared a previous time and space together. She spoke first, "Didn't you go to Palo Alto High School?"

"Yeah." He smiled. He remembered her by the far away look in her eyes. "We were in the same pre-calculus class. I'm Matt."

"What are you doing here?" she asked.

"I work here," he told her.

Before he had a chance to ask her the same question she started explaining. "My family is going on a cruise tomorrow. All around the Caribbean. How did you end up in Miami?"

"Hopped in my car and drove." He realized quickly that was an asshole answer. "I didn't really think things out. Just had to leave. A friend was heading here so I did too."

"That's awesome. So, you took a job here?"

"Yeah, I'm just building up life experiences. Maybe one day it will help me write the great American novel." He hated what he was saying. The first person who had taken any interest in his well being in a long time and he was speaking like a jerk. He tried to turn the conversation back to her. "What are you doing with yourself?"

"I graduated from UCLA and I'm working at a start-up back home in Palo Alto. It's pretty cool. We're trying to create a one stop domain where you can find people you have common interest with and connect..."

"Like a message board?"

"It will be more than that. We're hoping to be able to put video and songs and hey—didn't you used to write for the high school paper?"

"Yeah, I still do actually. Not the high school paper, but a newspaper in Davis. I write a weekly comic book column."

She started digging into her purse. She handed him her business card. Once he saw it in print, he remembered Austin was her name. "We could use content. We'll need writers, so maybe if you made it back to California it could be something. It doesn't pay much. Starting salary is only fifty k, but you'd get stock options, decent insurance."

"Fifty k? Like fifty thousand?"

"Yeah, I mean I know that's nothing, but it's all about the pay off if we make it. If it sounds like something you're interested in, shoot me an e-mail and we can talk more. I'll be back at work after New Year's."

He stared at the business card and a possible future. "Okay. Did you need help finding a book or anything?'

"Oh yeah, duh. It's like I talk about work and I get tunnel vision. I need this vacatiom. I'm looking for a book about the Caribbean."

He guided her to his domain that he manicured with very little care. "Aren't you guys, your start-up, aren't you worried about Y2K and like the end of civilization as we know it?"

"That's all bullshit."

"Really?"

"Yeah every generation thinks they're the important one, that in their lifetime is when it's all going to end. But life and humanity is going to keep going long after we're no longer here. This is it." She picked a book that was heavier on pictures than text. She quickly gave Matt a hug. "It was good to see you."

"You too. I'll send you an e-mail next millennium."

"Please do," she said as he stared deeply into the limited information her business card read.

December 24, 1999
Night Call

Jay told him they called it Noche Buena, it was a Christmas Eve party where they roasted a pig and drank a lot. Matt thanked him for the invite, but decided he did not want to go. It was kind for them to take him in, but tonight he knew being around other people would just make him feel lonelier.

He thought about sleeping. Maybe when he woke up Santa would have left him a present. Instead he heard the phone ring. He thought about not answering it. He knew it wasn't the debt collectors on the holiday, but he wasn't exactly sure who in the world he would want to talk to at this moment.

When he picked up the phone he was glad that he did. "Matt?"

"Hey, Erin," he answered.

"Merry Christmas," she said.

He looked at the clock to see if it was 12:00 yet. It wasn't, but he thought he would keep the tone jolly. "Merry Christmas to you. What's going on?"

"I just, you know, wanted to see how things are going. I stopped by your house today."

"Why did you do that?" he asked with a hint of anger.

"I thought maybe you were home. Your mom told me you were still in Florida, so I thought---"

"You talked to my mom?"

"Yeah. She invited me in. I saw your sister and dad too."

The thought of these festivities gave Matt an incredible sense of betrayal. "What did your boyfriend think of you hanging out with your ex's family?"

She sighed, "I'm not really seeing him any more."

He didn't say, "So that's why you're calling," but it was in the subtext of whatever he said next so much so that Erin said, "Sorry, I guess it wasn't cool of me to call."

"No, I'm glad," he said and he realized that he was happy to hear her voice. "You just woke me up. I was about to fall asleep."

"Oh, yeah, I guess it's kind of late out there."

"Not too late."

"How is it? I mean I've never spent a Christmas away from my family. Is it tough?"

"It's cool. I saved money on gifts." She didn't laugh. He went on. "I guess it's kind of weird. I've met some people out here through work and stuff and they're all nice, but it's the kind of relationship that if I died I don't think any of them would cry."

"That's a narcissistic way of looking at the world."

"I guess saying things like that isn't in the Christmas spirit."

"I'd cry if you died," she said.

"Thanks."

"My pleasure."

He went out to the balcony and looked up at the sky. There was the tiniest nip in the air, cold enough that he wished he wasn't barefoot. He wondered where exactly Santa Claus was right at that moment. There was a movie he saw as a kid that tried to explain the physics of how Santa could be at everyone's house exactly at midnight to deposit all the good children's gifts. Time as Matt remembered it magically stopped so Santa could make every child happy in one brief span of time. That was how it felt as their conversation fell into an easy rhythm. "I miss you," he finally said in a moment of weakness.

"I miss you too," she said.

He was able to stop himself from suggesting that they try to be together again. It would just lead to heartbreak when she told him next week over the phone she was back together with his replacement. Better to enjoy this moment of intimacy as it was in the present before he returned to his monastic lifestyle. If it was meant to be that they were to be back together than Father Christmas would make it happen. When the conversation hit a lull, he felt comfortable wishing her a merry Christmas one last time.

She did the same and they hung up.

He went back inside and saw it was 12:42 in the a.m. He thought about searching around the house for what Santa left him, but figured it would be better to wait until the morning.

December 25, 1999
Christmas Cheer

Matt screamed as he fell back on to the asphalt. Jay had given him a pair of rollerblades for Christmas. His elbow felt a little scratched up, but he figured he did pretty well to take almost an entire hour until he finally ate it.

When Jay brought the in-line skates over Matt felt awful that he didn't have anything to give his friend back. "You've given me plenty," Jay said. "Besides it's not like I paid for these."

Matt walked down the stairs and began to lace them up. He asked Jay if there were any pointers he could pass along.

"It's easy. If you ever ice skated it's the same motion. There's only one hard part to rollerblading." Matt didn't ask what it was so Jay nudged him to initiate the punchline, "Do you want to know what it is?"

"What?"

"Telling your dad, you're gay." As far as Matt could tell, the reason for Jay giving him this gift was not because the Christmas spirit had moved him, but was instead so that he could tell him that joke.

They skated down the street. At first Jay moved in a cautious, herky-jerky motion, but eventually found a fluidity. That was until he fell. But he blamed that act of clumsiness on getting tired and not on a lack of his feet knowing his way around the rollerblades. Matt rolled over to get into a sitting position as they watched the limited holiday crowd frolicking at John F. Kennedy Park.

"In one more week, it's all going to change."

2000 was starting to seem real. Last year around this time all Matt had to worry about was hearing the Prince song "1999" too many times, but this holiday season, mostly but not entirely due to the company Matt was keeping, was bringing other concerns. "How do you see it happening?" Matt asked Jay in all seriousness.

"It depends where you are. If you're out on the boat with me at midnight there won't be too much of a difference. If you're in a house out in the country away from things, you'll just have to deal with what would seem like an inconvenience of the power going out. But let's say you're in Times Square? Dick Clark is counting down and at one, the ball will drop, but so will a couple airplanes that fall out of the sky with their computers no longer working. The power will go out because the electric grid is all digitized. Subways might crash into each other. Newer cars with computers running their systems will halt leading to all kinds of crashes. Some people will run for cover and lock themselves up, others will take advantage of the chaos. They'll roam the streets taking what they think is rightfully theirs, and will be rightfully theirs since all of a sudden it will be survival of the fittest."

"And you'll be safe in the middle of the ocean?"

"I hope so. If you know a better place when civilization comes crashing down, tell me."

"For practical purposes I guess you're right."

"Damn straight I'm right. I'll catch fish for nutrition far away from the madness."

"I get that, but it just seems like if the world as we know it will end, it would be kind of sad to go through that alone."

"Come with me man, that's what I'm trying to tell you."

Matt politely declined the invitation knowing that if he was stranded on a boat alone with Jay for too long he might strangle him. "What about teaming up with Rasta Rick?"

"That fucker, he's why I've had to beg Mayra for her boat. He already took off to some cove in Jamaica that he said only the true Rastafari can enter. He's fucking nuts, that guy."

"This should come in handy," Matt said pointing at the rollerblades trying to change the subject. Jay had been seeming a little more unhinged as the calendar change approached.

"You've also got the bike. And your Peugeot is old enough it shouldn't have any computers in it, so that should run. Just make sure you fill up the tank and get a couple extra gallons because a lot of the fill up stations won't work without electricity. You could be okay, but you'll be safer on the boat."

"What are you going to do if there is no Y2K?" Matt asked. "If January 1, 2000 is exactly the same as December 31, 1999?"

"It won't be."

"But what if it is?"

"Then I guess I'll get a cell phone and an e-mail account and head on the pathway towards becoming a cyborg like everybody else."

The silence was almost awkward. Matt felt bad about ruining the holiday spirit. So he decided to make things festive again by telling his friend, "Merry Christmas, Jay."

"Merry Christmas, Matt."

December 28, 1999
You Never Really Know Someone

"Your friend is a maniac." Mayra said as Matt sat in the break room flipping through a British movie magazine telling him what movies to expect if we make it into the year 2000.

"I'm on break," Matt told her as he found the page he was looking for. They were making a movie about the X-Men for next summer. Maybe the world was going to end. After all of his childhood patiently waiting, they were finally making a movie based on a Marvel comic book. It must be the sign of Armageddon.

"Tell Jay to stop being such a creep."

"What's going on?" Matt asked though he was more interested in how the actors photographed corresponded with the drawings he had obsessed over.

"He keeps leaving me all of this whacked out poetry. Every day it's something weirder and freakier about how much he's in love with me."

Matt looked Mayra up and down trying to find some secret enclave of beauty within her physical form, he could not understand it. This was obviously some ploy that Jay was working to make sure he got that boat in the water. Matt of course did not want to share that information. Even if it would provide her comfort, it would later cause her pain. "Love makes men act in weird ways."

"He's just a fuck buddy," she informed Matt. "He can borrow the boat, but I'm sure as fuck not getting on there with that psycho."

She walked off leaving Matt a chance to start reading about a new *Mission Impossible* movie coming out. But out of the corner of his eye he saw she left the poem on the break table. He couldn't help himself but to read it, if for no other reason that to give Jay a hard time for being such a dog. It was titled, "Dearest Mayra"

Dearest Mayra
How I love ya
As I prepare to set sail
I pine to be your male

As the world will end
We can tend
To each other
You can be my Mother

And we will fuck
And fuck
And fuck
And fuck

Matt had to agree, it was pretty disturbing, or maybe just lazy. He couldn't rewrite it so he didn't have to call her his mother? Or maybe it was his sneaky way of getting her to give him the boat without having to deal with her? He kept going.

I'm always alone
Unless you phone
And share your day
Toward my way

Soon there will be
No electricity
Between each other
I will be your brother

And we will fuck
And fuck
And fuck
And fuck

That was it. Matt wanted to wash his hands after reading, but he only had a couple more minutes of break and he wanted to learn about the upcoming movie where Leonardo DiCaprio goes to Thailand.

December 31, 1999
One Last Chapter

Matt didn't believe Jay that it would work, but with merely a strong rope, his Peugeot was able to tow Mayra's boat all the way to the marina. Jay already proved more impressive with his seaworthiness than Matt would have given him credit for. Jay was even able to lower the boat down the ramp into the water with minimal damage.

"Sure you're going to be okay?" Matt asked.

"You're the one I'm worried about. You're not taking this seriously enough."

Matt had just expressed the same sentiments to Jay when he saw the minimal rations he was bringing. He loaded up at the health food store with about ten gallons of water, a bunch of granola he bought in bulk and a heavy stock of dried protein shake.

After the boat was completely stocked up Jay gave Matt another chance. "If everything goes to shit…"

"If?" Matt asked.

"When everything goes to shit meet me at the marina and I'll come back for you. On January 2 at ten a.m., I'm going to anchor right there." Jay pointed at a buoy. "Can you recognize this boat?"

"Yeah, it'll be the one with a hole in it that's sinking. You know you don't have to do this?" Matt told him. "Odds are nothing will happen and we'll all be just fine."

"That's two times in one sentence that you're wrong. Something always happens and none of us are making it out of here alive."

"Either way, if it's Doomsday or it it's just another weekday I'll come out here to see you the day after tomorrow at ten a.m."

"You're a good man, Matt." Jay gave Matt a hug. "A dumb man for taking your chances with society, but a good man." Jay hopped on to the boat and turned on the engine. It took several pulls but finally it purred and the boat sputtered away.

With the one percent or maybe ten percent chance that this might be the last time he ever saw Jay, Matt tried to express his gratitude. "Thanks for talking me into driving out here.'

With the noise or perhaps due to his concentration Jay did not seem to hear what Matt had to say. Matt almost yelled it again, but he figured it would be pointless. Barely a moment later Jay's borrowed vessel was curving out of the channel away from Matt's sightline.

Matt made the drive into work, what a fool he would feel if Jay was right. If this was their last chance with society as he knew it and instead of enjoying it he simply clocked in as if it was another day. Would this be his last chance to see a movie, write an e-mail, talk on the phone or even fly in a plane and he was spending it scanning merchandise with a laser and typing dollar amounts into a register?

But even if there was no paranoia in the air of what the next year and century and millennium might bring, this was not another day, it was New Year's Eve. All around the store there was talk of what to do. Mayra was having the party, with the store closing at 9 due to holiday hours. There was that buzz that was always present before a holiday, but this time it was louder and filled with suspense and a hint of dread.

At closing time Matt considered heading straight to the party, but he felt a little guilty about the fact that he might never again have contact with all the people he had ever told "I love you." So he headed home and called his parents first. There was no answer. He was about to hang up, but then decided he should leave a message. He told his parents and his sister that he loved them and that he hoped they had a wonderful New Year. Next he called Erin. Again, he left a voice mail. He told her he loved her and that he hoped they would find a way to see each other again in the year 2000.

Matt took a shower and changed his clothes. As he went into the fridge to pull out a six pack of beer for the party, he heard some stirring.

"Happy New Year, John!" Matt yelled out to his roommate who had made his way into the kitchen.

"Happy New Year," John repeated.

"Get dressed, man, there's a party."

"No, thank you. I think with the possibility of catastrophe, it's probably safer if I stay here."

"That's a shame. All this time I've lived with you, you still have never shown off those dancing moves you always brag about."

"I'm not bragging, I'm just describing factual information. I'm an exceptional dancer."

"Well maybe next year, right?" Matt did have one more question for John, something that had been bugging him since they first met. "Do you mind telling me what that secret job is that you do? I know it's confidential, but since the world might end tonight…"

Matt stopped speaking because John was looking around the apartment as though there might be another person listening in. When John seemed satisfied no one was, he replied. "I suppose I could tell you. I was working on the human genome project."

"Like you were studying human genes?"

"Yes, I was helping to diagram it, but I quit. I didn't like what I was learning. I really shouldn't tell you anything else."

"Okay then, well Happy New Year's, John."

"Happy New Year's to you," were the last words John spoke in the twentieth century. Matt closed the door. His first thought was what he always assumed when his roommate opened his mouth, that every word was a fabrication, either a lie or a delusion. But maybe it would make sense that uncovering what it means to be human would drive a man to madness or at the very least, oddness.

After a short drive Matt pulled up to Mayra's house, hoping for a satisfying last moment to the century. As he had to struggle to find an open spot to park, he could sense it was a bigger gathering than Mayra's other shindigs. He had to park a couple blocks away and didn't recognize a lot of the people there. The backyard looked quite different with all the people and one less boat.

The music was loud and the people were louder. This seemed like a good place to spend New Year's Eve. He wasn't entirely sure that this was where he would want to be during the end of the world, but hey. Either way Matt decided to start working on one of the beers as he looked around to find someone he knew. He walked toward a corner where he saw some of his co-workers when he was interrupted by a shout.

"Ten!" he heard someone yell.

This was happening earlier than he expected. Could there really be only a few seconds until nothing is ever the same again?

"Nine!"

Matt looked around. This was not the way he ever imagined the world could end, with everyone drunk and happy.

"Eight!"

If it is not the end, he should learn from this instance and treat life like the end was just around the corner. He decided if everything went smooth, tomorrow he would give Dan his two week notice that he was quitting.

"Seven!"

He would hop in his car and drive back home and take up that job offer where he could start off making fifty thousand a year. He could try to smooth things out with Erin. They could get married and have beautiful children together.

"Six!"

He kicked himself for thinking so far into the future again. He should be thinking about right now, because that's all we have. He told himself he would go kiss that pretty girl with the black lipstick at the end of the countdown.

"Five!"

Matt stopped heading towards the girl with black lipstick when he saw her kissing a guy who also seemed to be wearing black lipstick. He instead began to look for an escape route in case things fell apart right away. What would be worse? If something terrible were to happen at the end of the countdown or if nothing happened at all, that this was just another moment in a series of moments that make up our lives?

"Four!"

He wondered how Jay was doing out there in the middle of Biscayne Bay all alone. Maybe he should have been a good friend and gone with him.

"Three!"

He looked around at everyone filling up their cups with the cheapest champagne money could buy and wondered why he waited until now to appreciate it all. All the possibilities that the world had to offer. Would this be it? Would this be the end?

"Two!"

Or could he make this a glorious beginning?

"One!"

THE END